Edward Arber,   Virgil, Richard Stanyhurst

Translation of the First Four Books of the Aeneis of P. Virgilius Maro

with other poetical devices thereto annexed, June, 1582. Edited by Edward Arber

Edward Arber, Virgil, Richard Stanyhurst

Translation of the First Four Books of the Aeneis of P. Virgilius Maro
with other poetical devices thereto annexed, June, 1582. Edited by Edward Arber

ISBN/EAN: 9783337780265

Printed in Europe, USA, Canada, Australia, Japan

Cover: Foto ©Andreas Hilbeck / pixelio.de

More available books at **www.hansebooks.com**

𝕮𝖍𝖊 𝕰𝖓𝖌𝖑𝖎𝖘𝖍 𝕾𝖈𝖍𝖔𝖑𝖆𝖗'𝖘 𝕷𝖎𝖇𝖗𝖆𝖗𝖞 𝖔𝖋
𝕺𝖑𝖉 𝖆𝖓𝖉 𝕸𝖔𝖉𝖊𝖗𝖓 𝖂𝖔𝖗𝖐𝖘

RICHARD STANYHURST

Translation of the first Four Books

OF THE

Æneis of P. Virgilius Maro

with other poetical Devices
thereto annexed
[June] 1582

EDITED BY

EDWARD ARBER

F.S.A. ETC. LATE EXAMINER IN ENGLISH
LANGUAGE AND LITERATURE
TO THE UNIVERSITY OF
LONDON

WESTMINSTER

ARCHIBALD CONSTABLE AND CO.

1895

CONTENTS.

BIBLIOGRAPHY.

THE AUTHOR'S ORIGINAL TEXT, PRINTED AT LEYDEN.

ISSUE IN THE AUTHOR'S LIFETIME.

1. [June] 1582. Leyden, 4to. See title at p. 1.

After a long enquiry among the public Libraries of Holland and England, no nformation could be gained as to the existence of any copy of this impression. The only two copies now known are in private Collections: one at Ashburnham Place, Sussex; the other, at Britwell, in Bucks—each is slightly imperfect. By the great kindness of their possessors, Earl ASHBURNHAM and S. CHRISTIE-MILLER, Esq., it has been possible herein to give a perfect Text.

ISSUE SINCE HIS DEATH.

2 August, 1880. Willesden, London, N.W. 8vo. The present impression.

BINNEMAN'S REVISED TEXT, PRINTED BY HIM AT LONDON.

ISSUE IN THE AUTHOR'S LIFETIME.

2. [January] 1583. London, 8vo. See title at *p.* 159: and BINNEMAN's Address at *p.* 160. [Entered at Stationers' Hall on 24 January, 1583.]

ISSUE SINCE HIS DEATH.

3. 1836. Edinburgh, 4to. *The first four Bookes &c.* Edited by J[AMES] M[AIDMENT]. Fifty copies only printed.

Mr. MAIDMENT states at *p.* xv. that "no copy of" the Leyden Edition "has hitherto been traced."

⁂ *All former Editions were issued as separate Publications.*

INTRODUCTION.

I.

Y the kindness and public spirit of Earl ASHBURNHAM and S. CHRISTIE-MILLER, Esq., we are able to give back to the world, what is virtually the lost text of a work of great importance in our literary history, and especially in the history of English Verse.

For this translation of the *Æneid*, as it is one of the most audacious attempts at English hexameters, so it is among the very earliest printed specimens of them that appeared in our printed literature.

Dr. GABRIEL HARVEY writing, in his *Four Letters &c.* (on the 5th September 1592), with evident reference to his joint work with E. SPENSER which was registered at Stationers' Hall on 30 June 1580, and appeared under the title of *Three proper, and wittie, familiar Letters passed between two Vniuersitie men &c.*, exclaims.

If I neuer deserue anye better remembraunce, let mee rather be epitaphed. The Inuentour of the English Hexameter: whom learned M. *Stanihurst* imitated in his *Virgill*, and excellent Sir *Philip Sidney* disdained not to follow in his *Arcadia*, and elsewhere. *p.* 19.

Two years after to the very day, on the 30th June 1582, STANYHURST dedicates, at *p.* 10, this work to his brother-in-law Lord DUNSANY. So that HARVEY in the same *Foure Letters &c.*, thus mentions him, on the 8 September 1592, with other English hexametrists.

I cordially recommend to the deere Louers of the Muses: and namely to the professed Sonnes of the same ; *Edmond Spencer, Richard Stanihurst, Abraham France, Thomas Watson, Samuell Daniell, Thomas Nash*, and the rest : whome I affectionately thancke for their studious endeuours, commendably employed in enriching, and polishing their natiue Tongue, neuer so furnished, or embellished, as of late. *p.* 48.

I I.

HE best contemporary account we have met with of our Author, is from the bitterly hostile pen of that out and out Protestant, BARNABY RICH. It occurs, at *p.* 2, of his twenty-sixth book, *The Irish Hubbub,* [Preface dated 14 May] 1617.

And as the Irish are thus pleasantly conceited to iest and to scoffe, when they finde occasion, so they haue as great facility in weeping, as they haue in laughing, insomuch that one of their owne writers *Rychard Stanihurst* by name, a man of great esteeme among the Irish, famed for his learning and for his wisedome, they doe equall him to the seuen Sages of Greece, and doe think him worthy to be reputed for the eight'h' wise man.

It is truth, hee hath runne through diuers professions, first, for a lying learned Historiographer, hee hath shewed it in his Irish Chronicle.

After that he professed Poetry, and among other Fictions, he tooke vpon him to translate *Virgill,* and stript him out of a Veluet gowne, into a Fooles coate, out of a Latin Heroicall verse, into an English riffe raffe.

After that, I knew him at *Antwerp,* and there he professed Alchymy, and took vpon him to make Gold: from thence hee went to *Spaine,* and there hee became a Physition.

Now, I vnderstand, hee is in the Low Countries about the Arch Duke, and is there become a Massing Priest.

As we shall presently see that it was not till 1592, ten years after the appearance of these Poems, that STANYHURST went to Spain ; we must dissociate from *them* any idea of the Romish priesthood. At the time he wrote them, our Author was a learned Irish gentleman, living for his pleasure in the Low Countries. Presumably he was present at the death of his wife JANET on the 16th of August 1579 at Knightsbridge, *p.* 150. But, if so, he must have soon gone over to the Netherlands; and of these, to the Protestant Province of Holland : *i.e.,* to the Hague, where resided the brunette MARY, his platonic Mistress, whose "*vertu* meriteth more prayse, than parlye can vtter," *pp.* 141-143, 138-140 ; and to Leyden (eight years after its famous siege in 1574) during the printing of this book ; as PATES, at *p.* 157, pleading "thee absence of the author from perusing soom proofes," implies his presence at other times, which must have been a manifest necessity, on account of the extraordinary spelling.

Later on, he resided chiefly at Antwerp : and apparently never set foot again in either Ireland, the land of his birth ; or England, the home of his early manhood and brief married happiness.

III.

N the Seventh Chapter of his *Description of Ireland* in HOLINSHED's *Chronicles,* 1577, in enumerating *The names or surnames of the learned men and authors of Ireland,* our Author gives the following account of his parentage.

Nicholas Stanihurst ; he wrote in latine, *Dietam Medicorum. lib.* 1. He dyed in the yeare 1554.

James Stanihurst, late recorder of Dublyn, ouer hys exact knowledge in the common lawes, he was a good oratour, and a proper deuine.

He wrote in Englishe, beyng speaker in the parliamentes.

An oration made in the beginnyng of a parliament holden at Dublyn before the right honourable Thomas Erle of Sussex, &c., in the third and fourth yere of Philip and Mary [1557].

An oration made in the beginnyng of the parliament holden at Dublyn, before the right honourable Thomas Erle of Sussex, in the second yere of the raigne of our soueraigne lady Queene Elizabeth [1560].

An oration made in the beginnyng of a Parliament holden a Dublyn, before the right honourable sir Henry Sidney Knight, &c in the xj. yeare of the raigne of our soueraigne Lady Queene Elizabeth [1568.]

He wrote in Latin,
Pias Orationes.
Ad Corcaciensem decamem, epist. plures.

He deceased at Dublyn, the 27 of December [1573], being 51 yeres olde. Vpon whose death, I, as nature and duty bound me, made this epitaph. [*See it at p.* 148.]

Walter Stanihurst, sonne to James Stanihurst [*and brother to the writer*], he translated into English. *Innocent. de contemptu mundi.*

There flourished before any of these a Stanihurst, that was a scholer of Oxford, brother to Genet Stanihurst, *Circa annum* a famous and ancient matrone of Dublyn, she lieth *dom.* 1506. buried in S. Michaels church. [*p.* 27.]

None of these several writings appear to have been printed.

IV.

NTHONY À WOOD's account of our Author's education is as follows:—

RICHARD STANYHURST, son of JAMES STANYHURST, Esq., was born within the city of Dublin in Ireland (of which city his father was then recorder), educated in grammar learning under PETER WHYTE, became a commoner of University College Oxford in 1563, where improving those rare natural parts that he was endowed with [in 1565], wrote "Commentaries on PORPHYRY." [*Harmonia seu Catena Dialectica in Porphyrum.* Londini, 1570 and 1579 fol.; Ludguni, fol.; and Parisus, 4to. *Sir J. WARE, Works* ii. 98. *Ed.* 1745. *fol.* at two years standing, being then 18 years of age, to the great admiration of learned men and others. After he had taken *on 7 June 1567, see Fasti Oxon.* ii. 179. *Ed.* 1815 one degree in arts, he left the college, retired to London, became first a student in Furnival's Inn, where spending some time in the study of the common law, he afterwards went into the country of his nativity for a time.

Principles of Cath. Religion.—This I haue not yet seen, and therefore I cannot tell you when, or where it was printed. .

But as for the epitaph of our author, (which he should haue made while living) none doth appear at Dublin, neither at Brussels, (as I can yet learn,) where he died in 1618. *Athenæ Oxon.* ii. 252. *Ed.* 1815.

V.

UR Author only published three English works. The *Description of Ireland*, and the *History of Ireland*, lib. iii. (that is, during the reign of HENRY VIII. only, referred to at *pp.* 146-147); both of which appeared in the First Volume of RAPHAEL HOLINSHED's *Chronicles* in 1577: and the present volume of Poems and Translations. Everything else, apparently, he wrote in Latin.

As his style is almost a matter of wonderment, it will be useful to give the first piece of his English ever published; his *Epistle* to Sir HENRY SIDNEY, the Lord Deputy of Ireland before his *Description*, in 1577. It will also show that the peculiar oddities of thought were natural to him from the first, and were not specially studied for this Volume, which did not appear till five years later, in 1582.

MY VERY GOOD LORDE,

Here haue beene diuers of late, that with no small toyle, and great commendacion, haue throughly imployed themselues, in culling and packing togither the scrapings and fragments of the Hystorie of

Ireland. Among which crew, my fast friende, and inwarde compagnion, M. Edmond Campion, dyd so learnedly bequite himselfe, in the penning of certayne briefe notes, concerning that countrey, as certes it was greatly to be lamented, that eyther hys theame had not beene shorter, or else his leasure had not beene longer.

For if Alexander were so rauisht with *Homer* hys historie, that notwithstanding *Thersites* were a crabbed and rugged dwarfe, being in outwarde feature so deformed, and in inwarde conditions so crooked, as he seemed to stande to no better steede, than to lead Apes in hell, yet the valiaunt capitayne weighing, howe liuely the golden Poet set foorth the ougly dandeprat in his colours, dyd sooner wyshe to be *Homer* his *Thersites*, then to be the Alexander of that doltish rythmour, which vndertooke, with his woodden verses to blase his famous and martiall exploytes : howe much more ought Irelande (being in sundry ages seized of diuers good and couragious Alexanders) sore to long, and thirste after so rare a clarcke, as M. Campion, who was so vpright in conscience, so deepe in iudgement, so rype in eloquence, as the countrey might haue bene wel assured, to haue had their hystorie truly reported, pithily handled, and brauely polished.

Howbeit, although the glose of his fine abridgement, being matcht with other mens dooings, bare a surpassing kinde of excellencie, yet it was so hudled vp in haste, as in respect of a Campion his absolute perfection, it seemed rather to be a work roughly hewed, then smoothly planed. Vpon which grounde the gentleman being willing, that his so tender a suckling, hauing as yet but greene bones, should haue beene swadled and rockt in a cradle, till in tract of tyme the ioynctes thereof were knit, and growen stronger, yet notwithstanding he was so crost in the nycke of thys determination, that his hystorie in mitching wyse wandred through sundry hands, and being therwithall in certaine places somewhat tyckle tongued (for M. Campion dyd learne it to speake) and in other places ouer spare, it twitled more tales out of schoole, and drowned weightyer matters in silence, then the Autor vpon better view, and longer searche woulde haue permitted.

Thus much being by the sager sorte pondered, and the perfection of the hystorie earnestly desired, I, as one of the most, that could doe least, was fully resolued, to enriche M. Campion his *Chronicle*, with further additions. But weighing on the other side, that my course pack threede coulde not haue beene sutetably knit with his fine silcke, and what a disgrace it were, hungerly to botch vp a ritche garment, by clowting it with patches of sundrye coulours, I was forthwyth reclaymed from my former resolution, reckening it for better, that my penne shoulde walke in such wyse in that craggie and balkishe way, as the truth of the matter being forepriced, I would neyther openly borrow, nor priuely imbezell, ought to any great purpose from his historie.

But as I was hammering that worke by stealthes on ye anuille, I was giuen to vnderstande by some of mine acquaintance, that others had brought our rawe hystorie to that rypenesse as my paine therein, woulde seeme but needelesse. Wherevpon being willing to be eased of the burden, and loath also in lurching wise to forestall any man his trauayle, I was contented, to leaue them thumping in the forge, and quietlye to repayre to mine vsuall and pristinate studies, taking it not to stande with good maners, lyke a flittering flye, to fall in an other man his dishe.

Howbeit, the little payne I tooke therin was not so secretly mewed within my closet, but it slipt out at one chincke or other, and romed so farre abroade, as it was whispered in their eares, who before were in the hystorie busied. The gentlemen conceyuing a greater opinion of mee, then I was well able to vpholde, dealt very effectually with mee, that as well at their instaunce, as for the affection I bare to my natiue countrey, I woulde put mine helping hand, to the building and perfecting of so commendable a worke. Hauing breathed for a fewe dayes on this motion, albeit I knewe, that my worke was plumed with Downe, and at that time, was not sufficientlye feathered to flee, yet I was by them weighed not to beare my selfe coy, by giuing mine entier friendes in so reasonable a request a squaimish repulse.

Wherefore, my singular good Lorde, here is layde downe to your Lordshippe his view a briefe *discourse*, with a iagged *hystorie* of a ragged Weale publicke. Yet as naked as at the first blushe it seemeth, if it shall stande wyth your Honour his pleasure (whome I take to be an experte Lapidarie) at vacant houres to insearche it, you shall finde therein stones of such estimation, as are woorthy to be coucht in riche and precious collets. And in especiall your Lordship, aboue all others, in that you haue the charge of that countrey, may here be schooled, by a right line to leuell your gouernement.

For in perusing this hystorie, you shall finde vice punished, vertue rewarded, rebellion suppressed, loyaltie exalted, hautinesse dislyked, courtisie beloued, brybery detested, iustice embraced, polling Officers to their perpetuall shame reprooued, and vpright gouernours to their eternall fame extolled.

And truely, to my thinking, such magistrates, as meane to haue a vigilant eye to their charge, can not bestow their tyme better, then when they sequestre themselues from the affayres of the wealpublicke, to recreate and quicken their spirites by reading the Chronicles, that decipher the gouernement of a wealepublicke. For as it is no small commendacion, for one to beare the dooings of many, so it breedeth great admiration, generally to haue all those qualities in one man herboured, for which particularly diuers are eternized. And who so will be addicted to the reading of hystories, shall readily finde diuers euentes woorthy to be remembred, and sundry sounde examples daily to be followed.

Vpon which grounde the learned haue, not without cause, adiudged an historie to be, the Marrowe of reason, the creame of experience, the sappe of wysedoome, the pith of iudgement, the library of knowledge, the kernell of pollicie, the vnfoldresse of treacherie, the kalender of tyme, the lanterne trueth, the lyfe of memorie, the doctresse of behauiour, the register of antiquitie, the trumpet of chiualrie.

And that our Irishe hystorie being diligently heeded, yeeldeth al these commodities, I trust the indifferent reader, vpon the vntwyning thereof, will not denie. But if any man his stomacke shall be founde so tenderly niced, or so deintily spyced, as that he may not, forsooth, digest the grose draffe of so base a countrey, I doubt not, but your Lordship, who is throughly acquaynted with the woorthinesse of the Island, will be soone perswaded, to leaue such quaint and licourous repastours, to feede on their costly and delicate Woodcockes, and willingly to accept the louing present of your hearty welwiller.

The gift is small, the giuer hys good wyll is great, I stand in good hope, that the greatnesse of the one wyll counterpoise the smalnesse of the other. Wherefore, that I may the sooner vnbroyde ye pelfish trash, that is wrapt wythin thys

Treatise, I shall craue your Lordshippe, to lende me eyther your eares in hearing, or your eyes in reading the tenour of the discourse following.

To these two English works on Ireland, STANYHURST, in 1584, added a third in Latin : *De rebus in Hibernia gestis. lib. iv.*, dealing with its early history down to the time of Henry II. ; with an Appendix of annotated extracts from GIRALDUS Cambrensis. This work was printed at Antwerp, and its title page states *Omnia nunc primum in lucem edita.* Camden in his *Britannia*, 600, Ed. 1586, describing the country of West Meath, alludes to our Author as *Eruditissimus ille nobilis Richardus Stanihurstus.*

It is, in reference to all three works, that G. KEATING, D.D. in his *General History of Ireland, p.* xii. *Ed.* 1723, states, that, for three unanswerable reasons, STANYHURST was utterly unfitted to write a Chronicle. 1. He was too young when he wrote. 2. He was ignorant of Erse. 3. That being bribed [*as Doctor KEATING avers*] by large gifts and promises of advancement upon condition that he would blacken the Irish nation, he had renounced the impartiality necessary to a historian. The Doctor then adds

But he lived to repent of the Injustice he had been guilty of, and when afterwards he enter'd into holy Orders, he promis'd by a formal Recantation publickly to revoke all the Falshoods he had recorded in that Work ; and for that Purpose (as I am credibly inform'd) a Writing was drawn up in order to be printed in *Ireland* and laid before the whole World ; but, if it was ever publish'd, I could never find a Copy of it, and therefore an apt to believe that it was by some Means or other utterly suppressed.

Sir JAMES WARE, in the First Book of his *Writers of Ireland* (ii. 98. of his *Works*, Ed. 1745, fol.) thinks that Doctor KEATING falls foul of these four books *De rebus, &c.* "with some reason, if it be considered with what numbers of errors, not to say malicious representations it abounds."

From these testimonies it would appear that STANYHURST as an Historian, and probably in all his other sympathies not influenced by his religion, represents more the Englishry in Ireland than the native Celt.

V I.

BEING of the Englishry in Ireland, it came about that our Author was Uncle to Archbishop USHER ; in whose *Life* by R. PARR, D.D. his chaplain and literary executor, 1686, fol. he is thus referred to.

JAMES USHER was born in the City of Dublin, the metropolis of Ireland, on the fourth day of January A.D. 1580.

His father, Master ARNOLD USHER, one of the six Clerks of Chancery, and of good repute for his prudence and integrity, was of the ancient family of the USHERS *alias* NEVILS, whose ancestor, Usher to King John, coming over with him into Ireland, and setling there, change the name of his Family into that of his Office, as was usual in that age. His descendants have since branched into several families about Dublin, and, for divers ages, bore the most considerable Offices, in and about that city.

His mother was Margaret, daughter of James Stanihurst, who was of considerable note in his time, being chosen Speaker of the Honourable House of Commons in three [Irish] Parliaments, and was Recorder of the City of Dublin, and one of the Masters in Chancery : and that, which ought always to be mentioned for his honour, he was the First Mover, in the last of the three [Irish] Parliaments of Queen Elizabeth, for the founding and endowing of a College and University at Dublin; which was soon after consented to by Her Majesty.

His uncle, by his mother's side, was Richard Stanihurst, a learned man, of the Romish persuasion, an excellent historian, philosopher, and poet. One of whose works [Brevis Præmunitio], for that reason, written against his nephew; yet notwithstanding their difference in judgement, they had frequent correspondence by letters.

The first letter in this Volume is an undated one [but about 1610] from Usher to "Master Richard Stanihurst at the English College in Louvain," thus begins and ends.

Dear Uncle,
Having the opportunity of this messenger so fitly offered unto me, I make bold to desire your furtherance in some matters that concern my studies. . . .

Your own treatise of St. Patrick's Life I have; as also your Hebdomada Maria. Your Margarita Mariana, and other writings (if there be any) I have much sought for, but could not as yet get. Thus presuming on that natural bond of love which is knit betwixt us, that I shall receive such satisfaction from you as I expect; with my mother, your sister's most kind remembrance, I remain
Your most loving Nephew,
James Usher.

Among Robert Turner's Collection of Orationes, Epistilæ &c. of E. Campian, Ingoldstat, 1602, 8vo, are three Latin letters to R. Stanyhurst. The first dated St. John's College, Calendris Decembris, 1570, praising his Harmonia &c. The other two dated "Turvio 13. Cal. April 1571."

VII.

OUR Author's third and his most famous English Work, was his translation of the *Æneid.*

In October 1587, he dedicated, at Antwerp, to the Duke of PARMA,
his *De Vita S. Patricii Hiberniæ Apostoli, lib. ii.*

Among the letters to JUSTUS LIPSIUS, which a represerved in the First
Volume of *Sylloges Epistolarum* by PETER BURMANN the Elder (published at
Leyden, 1724, 4to), are two which fix STANYHURST's visit to Spain in 1591–1592.
The first letter (*p.* 93) is from A. C. LEIVA, is dated Toleti, *A.D. xi. Kal. Septembr*
1592, and contains the following passage :

Quare potes facile intelligere, quam optatæ, quam gratæ quam
et jucundæ tuæ illæ literæ acciderint, quas ad D. RICHARDUM
STANIHURSTUM, Vir Nobilem dedisti, missas mihi a D. JOANNE
SILVA.

The second (*p.* 602) is from STANYHURST himself, and is dated, Madridi *Calend.*
Februarii 1592.   It contains the following passage :

Patuit mihi, statim fere atque Madridum perveni, ad Regem
Catholicum non modo aditus, sed etiam introitus.   Bone
DEVS, quanta in potentissimo orbis terrarum Monarcha comitas
adfabilitasque sermonis ?

Sir JAMES Ware (*Works,* ii. 98. *Ed.* 1745) states

Our Author, RICHARD, had a Son named WILLIAM STANI-
HURST, who was born at *Brussels* in 1601, and at the Age of
Sixteen entred into the Society of the Jesuits.   He was a
Man endowed with excellent Parts, and a Writer of several
Treatises, of which SOTVELLUS gives a Catalogue.   He died
on the 10th of January 1663.

It is clear that the Poet had not entered the Priesthood at this date : because to
RICHARD VERSTEGAN's *Restitution of Decayed Intelligence,* printed at Antwerp
about February 1605, but also sold in London, he contributed a prefatory twelve-
line Latin *Carmen,* under his old designation of *Dublinensis.*

So that it was only when he was about sixty years of age, and some twenty-five
years after the publication of these Translations, that he became a priest ; and
being an eminent man, he is made a Chaplain to the Austrian Archduke ALBERT
and his wife ; and thus his next publication, *Hebdomada Mariana in memoriam*
septem festorum Virg. MARIÆ, per singulos hebdomadæ dies distributæ, printed, in
8vo, at Antwerp, in 1609, he designates himself *Serenissorum principum Sacellanus.*
This is the work referred to by USHER above.

Five years later, he published his *Hebdomada eucharistica,* Duaci 1614, 8vo.
Archbishop USHER's celebrated work, *De Ecclesiarum Christianarum Succes-*

sione et Statu appeared in **1613**, and naturally elicited from his Uncle what appears to have been his last work.

Brevis præmunitio pro futura concertatione cum IACOBO VSSERIO Hibernio Dubliniensi, qui in sua historica explicatione conatur probare, Pontificem Romanum (legitimum CHRISTI, in terris, Vicarium) verum et germanum esse ANTICHRISTUM. Duaci. 1615.

Three years later, according to WOOD, he died at Brussels.

VIII.

HERE remains now the consideration of STANYHURST as an English Poet; his principal claim for which is based upon the present Text. And first, for Contemporary Criticism.

The *Æneid* was translated under the combined influence of Sir THOMAS MORE, THOMAS PHAER, ROGER ASCHAM, and GABRIEL HARVEY; only the second of whom could, in any sense, be considered a Poet. Of these, HARVEY was the only one now alive; and he speedily glorified, as we have seen at *p.* xii., the method, the execution, and the Author.

Ascham, in his *Scholemaster,* 1570 (which STANYHURST, at *p.* 4, calls "his goulden pamphlet"), treating of *Imitatio,* thus expresses the mind of Sir JOHN CHEKE, Bishop THOMAS WATSON, and himself, on the subject of Rhyme. Again we say, they were not English poets.

This matter maketh me gladly remember my sweet tyme spent at Cambrige, and the pleasant talke which I had oft with *M. Cheke* and *M. Watson* [*i.e., in Henry VIII's reign*], of this fault, not onely in the olde Latin Poets, but also in our new English Rymers at this day. They wished [that] as *Virgil* and *Horace* were not wedded to follow the faultes of former fathers (a shrewd mariage in greater matters) but by right *Imitation* of the perfit Grecians, had brought Poetrie to perfitnesse also in the Latin tong, that we Englishmen likewise would acknowledge and vnderstand rightfully our rude beggerly ryming, brought first into Italie by *Gothes* and *Hunnes,* when all good verses and all good learning to, were destroyed by them: and after caryed into France and Germanie: and at last receyued into England by men of excellent wit in deede, but of small learning, and lesse judgement in that behalfe.

In deed, our English tong, hauing in vse chiefly, wordes of one syllable which commonly be long, doth not well receiue the nature of *Carmen Heroicum,* bicause *dactylus,* the aptest foote for that verse, conteining one long and two short, is seldom therefore found in English: and doth also rather stumble than stand upon *Monasyllabis. Quintilian* in hys learned Chapiter *de Compositione*, geueth this lesson *de Monasyllabis,* before me : and in the same place doth iustlie inuey against all Ryming, if there be any, who be angrie with me for misliking of Ryming, may be angry for company to, with *Quintilian* also, for the same thing: And yet *Quintilian* had not so iust cause to mislike of it than, as men haue at his day.

And though *Carmen Exametrum* doth rather trotte and hoble, than runne smothly in our English tong, yet I am sure, our English tong will receive *carmen Iambicum* as naturallie, as either *Greke* or *Latin.*   *p.* 145. *Ed.* 1870.

Toм Nash, in his first work, the *Preface* to Greene's *Menaphon* August, 1589, which is to our felicity to republish in this Series, on the same day as the present Work, thus criticizes this performance.

But fortune the Mistres of change with a pitying compassion, respecting Master *Stanihursts* praise, would that *Phaer* shoulde fall that hee might rise, whose heroicall Poetrie infired, I should say inspired, with an hexameter furie, recalled to life, whateuer hissed barbarisme, hath bin buried this hundred yeare ; and reuiued by his ragged quill, such carterlie varietie, as no hodge plowman in a countrie, but would haue held as the extremitie of clownerie ; a patterne whereof, I will propounde to your iudgements, as neere as I can, being parte of one of his descriptions of a tempest, which is this

Then did he make, heauens vault to rebounde, with rounce robble hobble
Of ruffe raffe roaring, with thwick thwack thurlery bouncing [See p. 138.]

Which strange language of the firmament neuer subiect before to our common phrase, makes vs that are not vsed to terminate heauens moueings, in the accents of any voice, esteeme of their triobulare interpreter, as of some Thrasonical huffe snuffe, for so terrible was his stile, to all milde eares, as would haue affrighted our peaceable Poets, from intermedling hereafter, with that quarrelling kinde of verse ; had not sweete Master *France* by his excellent translation of Master *Thomas Watsons* sugred *Amintas*, animated their dulled spirits, to such high witted endeuors.

Three years later, in this *Strange News*, 1592, Nash again refers to the present work.

Master *Stannyhurst* (though otherwise learned) trod a foule lumbering boystrous wallowing measure in his translation of *Virgil.*   He had neuer been praisd by *Gabriel* [*Harvey* for his his labour, if therein hee had not bin so famously absurd.   G.3.

GEORGE PUTTENHAM, in his *Arte of English Poesie*, 1589, thus refers to our Author, among

Such makers as haue sought to bring into our vulgar Poesie some of the auncient feete, to wit, the *Dactile* into verses *exameters*, as he that translated certaine bookes of *Vergils Eneydos* in such measures and not uncommendably. Book II. c. xii.

He also appears to refer to our Author's use of the words *trudge* and *tugge* at *p.* 17, while treating of Decorum in speech.

And yet in speaking or writing of a Princes affaires and fortunes there is a certaine *Decorum*, that we may not vse the same termes in their busines, as we might very wel doe in a meaner persons, the case being all one, such reuerence is due to their estates. . . . As one, who translating certaine bookes of *Virgils Æneidos* into English meetre, said that *Æneas* was fayne to trudge out of Troy : which terme became better to be spoken of a beggar, or of a rogue, or of a lackey : for so wee vsed to say to such maner of people, *be trudging hence.*

The same translatour when he came to these wordes : *Insignem pietate virum, tot voluere casus tot adire labores compulit.* Hee turned it thus, what moued *Iuno* to *tugge so great a captaine* as *Æneas*, which word *tugge* spoken in this case is so vndecent as none other coulde haue bene deuised, and tooke his first originall from the cart, because it signifieth the pull or draught of the oxen or horses, and therefore the leathers that beare the chiefe stresse of the draught, the cartars call them tugges, and so wee vse to say that *shrewd boyes tugge each other by the eares*, for *pull.*   Book III. c. xxiii.

FRANCIS MERES, M.A., in his *Palladis Tamia*, [September] 1598, says

Amongst vs I name but two Iambical poets, *Gabriel Harvey* and *Richard Stanyhurst*; because I haue seen no more in this kind.

JOSEPH HALL, who was Bishop of NORWICH, in his *Virgidemiarum*, 1597, consecrates the Sixth Satire of his First Book to STANYHURST.

NOTHER scorns the home-spun threed of rimes,
Match'd with the loftie feet of elder times :
Giue him the numbred verse that *Virgil* sung,
And *Virgill* selfe shall speake the English tung :
Manhood and garboiles shall he chaunt [*p.* 17] with chaunged feete,
And head-strong *Dactils* making Musicke meete.

The nimble *Dactils* striuing to out-go
The drawling *Spondees* pacing it below.
The lingring *Spondees*, labouring to delay,
The breath-lesse *Dactils* with a sudden stay.
Who euer saw a colt wanton and wilde,
Yok'd with a slow-foote oxe on fallow field?
Can right arced how handsomly besets
Dull *Spondees* with the English *Dactilets*?
If *Ioue* speake English in a thundring cloud,
Thwick thwack [p. 138], and *Rif raf* p. 21], rores he out aloud.
Fie on the forged mint that did create
New coyne of words neuer articulate.

In 1599, an out and out Hexametrist, published, in a small oblong shape, *The First Booke of the Preservation of King Henry the VII., when he was but Earle of Richmond, Grandfather to the Queenes maiesty.* Compiled in english rythmicall Hexameters.

In this work, besides a praise of our Author, there is an interesting piece of contemporary poetical criticism.

Right honored, worshipfull, and gentell Reader, these Hexa-meters and Pentameters in Englishe, are misliked of many, because they are not yet come to their full perfection: and specially of some, that are accounted and knowne to be Doctors and singularly well learned and great Linguistes: but especially of the plaine Rythmer, that scarce knowes the footed quantitie or metricall scanning thereof; muche lesse to reade them with a grace according to the same. But for him, I say thus; Scientia nullum habet inimicum, præter ignorantem. *Whose bookes are stuft with lines of prose, with a rythme in the end; which euery fidler, or piper, can make vpon a theame giuen. Neuerthelesse, I confesse and acknowledge that we haue many excellent and singular good Poets in this our age, as Maister* Spencer, *that was, Maister* Gowlding, *Doctor* Phayer, *Maister* Harrington, Daniell, *and diuers others whom I reuerence in that kinde of prose-rythme: wherein* Spencer *(without offence spoken) hath surpassed them all. I would to God they had done so well in trew Hexameters: for they had then beautified our language. For the* Greekes *and* Latines *did in a manner abolish quite that kinde of rythme-prose: And why should not we doe the like in Englishe? . . . .*

Therefore I reuerence Stanihurst; *who, being but an Irish man, did first attempt to translate those foure bookes of* Eneados, *which*

(if he be liuing) I desire him to refile them ouer againe; and
thus haue written in verses.

> If the Poet Stanihurst *yet liue and feedeth on ay-er,*
> *I do request him (as one that wisheth a grace to the meter)*
> *With wordes significant to refile and finely to polishe*
> *Those fower Æneis, that he late translated in English.*
> *I doe the man reuerence, as a fine, as an exquisit Author:*
> *For that he first did attempt, to translate verse as a Doctor.*

For at the first, Maister Askam *had much ado to make two or*
three verses in English : but now euery scholler can make some.
What language so hard, harsh, or barbarous, that time and art
will not amend ? . . . .

This trew kinde of Hexametred and Pentametred verse, will
bring vnto vs foure commodities. First it will enrich our speach
with good and significant wordes : Secondly it will bring a delight
and pleasure to the skilfull Reader, when he seeth them formally
compyled : And thirdly it will incourage and learne the good and
godly Students, that affect Poetry, and are naturally enclyned
thereunto, to make the like : Fourthly it will direct a trew Idioma,
and will teach trew Orthography. For as gould surpasseth leade :
so the Hexameters surpasse rythme prose.

IX.

F **LATER** opinions concerning our Poet, we may quote the following :

THOMAS WHARTON, B.D., refers to this Translation in his *History of English Poetry,* iii. 399. *Ed.* 1781. (iv. 284, *Ed.* 1871.)

[ROBERT SOUTHEY, in] *Omniana or Horæ Otiosiores,* i. 193. *Ed.* 1812.

As Chaucer has been called the well of English undefiled, so might Stanihurst be denominated the common sewer of the language. He is, however, a very entertaining, and to a philologist, a very instructive writer. His version of the four first books of the *Æneid* is exceedingly rare, and deserves to be reprinted for its incomparable oddity. It seems impossible that a man could have written in such a style without intending to burlesque what he was about, and yet it is certain that STANIHURST seriously meant to write heroic poetry.

The present United States Minister to Italy, his Excellency GEORGE P. MARSH, has some remarks on our author, in his *Origin and History of the English Language.* p. 538, *Ed.* 1862.

Notices of the present Text also occur in *Censura Literaria,* ii. and iv. *Ed.* 1806–7; in HALLAM's *Introduction to the Literature of Europe,* II., c. v., p. 131.

Ed. 1854; and in Mr. C. C. FELTON's article in *North American Review,* July 1846, lxiii., 157, n., and others, with references to Mr. MAIDMENT's reprint, in *Gentleman's Magazine,* 1844. ii. 603; and COLLIER's *Bibliographical and critical Account &c.* ii., 386, *Ed.* 1865.

X.

E HAVE bestowed extraordinary care on the absolutely faithful reproduction of the Leyden text in its integrity, not referring to the London text at all, because BINNEMAN states, *p.* 160, that he had "here and there changed some one or other letter." For two months, Lord ASHBURNHAM's volume was at our service at the house of the Society of Antiquaries, in the charge of C. KNIGHT WATSON, Esq., F.S.A., the Secretary; and Mr. S. CHRISTIE-MILLER's copy at the British Museum, in the care of R. E. GRAVES, Esq. Both Mr. WATSON and Mr. GRAVES most obligingly rendered every facility in the matter.

XI.

EAVING the merits of the following Translations regarded as versions of their several originals, to the discussion of others : we can here only say a few words on STANYHURST's English. First, on the words themselves ; next, on the use he made of them.

1. One may say of him, that he, at any rate, had the courage of his convictions ; that he, at least, had not the fear of man before his eyes, when he set to work to torture the English language. As utterly reckless in his English spelling as ever the Rev. CHARLES BUTLER, Vicar of Wotton, was, and far more so than JAMES HOWELL ; he will, doubtless, be revered as a Forerunner, by the Spelling Reformers of this and coming ages : but his labours were useless and thrown away, as theirs will also be. With that universal and perpetual abrasion of words, known as the Law of Economy of Speech, daily in operation before our eyes, is not all language sufficiently full of changes already?

Now, we are able to trace in its present remains, the history of a word through a thousand years. The arbitrary introduction of any partial or entire mathematical formulæ for the representation of human speech, like Bishop WILKINS' *Real Character,* would destroy this. If our Spelling Reformers go not so far as this : why should they advocate a theoretical arrangement of consonants and vowels on the Phonetic basis : when the theory on which they would have us base the change, may be out of date in fifty years hence ; and must rest too, on a perpetual Universal Consent, of which they can never assure themselves. What have our American friends gained by spelling traveller with one *l,* but the sense that every time they write it so, they have stamped a good word with the badge of illegitimacy. Let the changes in spelling that inevitably will come, come of themselves, and as it were unconsciously.

We will just gather a mere sample or handful of some of the extraordinary things in this Text ; putting them under the headings of **1. Letters. 2. Words. 3. Affixes. 4. Mimetics** *and* **Alliteration.** And **5. Phrases** *and* **Proverbs.** The references to the pages are in no sense exhaustive.

1. Letters.

ERRATIC SPELLING.

AGGLUTINATED WORDS.

DISSEVERED WORDS.

2. Words.

FRENCH WORDS.

WORDS NOT YET ACCLIMATIZED IN ENGLISH.

3. Affixes.

UNUSUAL PREFIXES.

UNUSUAL SUFFIXES.

4. Mimetics *and* Alliterations.

TWO MIMETIC WORDS ONLY.

MIMETIC SENTENCES.

Theese flaws theyre cabbans with stur snar iarrye doe ransack...	19
Lyke bandog grinning, with gnash tusk greedelye snarring	27
Lyke wrastling meete winds with blaste contrarius huzing	57
Whear curs barck bawling, with yolp yalpe snarrye rebounding	84

ALLITERATION

Is very frequent, as swage seas surging	19
prittye parrat prating	26
ragd rocks rustye	88
a foul fog pack paunch	101

5. Phrases *and* Proverbs.

We give a few specimens of these just as they meet us.

Somewhat nappy of the spigget ...	4	To find a horse nest	14
Break the ice	5	If this gear cotten...	19
Altogether in a wrong box	5	Stand ye to your tacklings	24, 88, 115
Stand nicely on my pantofles ...	5	All cock sure	36
Slice the husk, and crack the shell	6	In straw there lurketh some pad...	39
Pry out a pimple in a bent	6	I like not barrel or herring	45
The fat were in the fire	6	Like a wayward obstinate old grey	
The market were marred	6	[horse]	64
Forelittring bitches whelp blind		Paltock's Inn	72
puppies	8	"Scarborough warning"	81
Peale meale	9	Scarborough scrabling	116
Not worth a bean	10	True tales vainly to twattle	101
Blind bayards rush on forward ...	10	As wild as a March hare	101
Miss the cushion	12	From post to pillar	104
Some grammatical pullet clocking		Stand at a deadlift	155
against me	14	Hit the nail on the head	155

2. But what is more remarkable is the use to which STANYHURST applied these and such like materials. He employed these common words and sayings, this "kitchen rhetoric," in the expression of an Epic Story ! and that, purposely ; and also, probably, in good faith. The result is that, with all its sound and fury, his translation is perhaps the most irresistibly comic of all English Versions of the *Æneid* ; and can scarcely ever be read without shouts of laughter.

Important as it is to the history of English hexameter verse ; there is ever this strong personal flavour of oddity and grotesqueness, which enables us to see that this hitherto lost Text was intrinsically a very remarkable book in our Elizabethan literature.

XII.

S WE began, so will we conclude, by expressing our thanks to Lord ASHBURNHAM and S. CHRISTIE-MILLER, Esq., for the pleasure they have given to all cultivated persons in facilitating the present impression by the loan of their precious originals.

THEE FIRST FOV-
RE BOOKES OF VIR-
GIL HIS AENEIS TRANSLA-
ted intoo English heroical verse by Ri-

chard Stanyhurst, wyth oother

Poëtical diuises there-

too annexed.

Imprinted at Leiden in Holland by Iohn Pates.

Anno M. D. LXXXII.

TOO THEE RIGHT

HONOVRABLE MY

VERIE LOOVING BROO-
THER THEE LORD BA-
RON OF DVNSANYE.

Hat deepe and rare poynctes of hydden secrets *Virgil* hath sealde vp in his twelue bookes of *Æneis*, may easelye appeere too such reaching wyts, as bend theyre endewours, too thee vnfolding thereof; not onlye by gnibling vpon thee outward ryne of a supposed historie, but also by groaping thee pyth, that is shrind vp wythin thee barck and bodye of so exquisit and singular a discourse. For where as thee chiefe prayse of a wryter consisteth in thee enterlacing of pleasure wyth profit : oure author hath so wiselye alayed thee one wyth thee oother, as thee shallow reader may bee delighted wyth a smooth tale, and thee diuing searcher may bee aduantaged by sowning a pretiouse treatise. And certes this preheminencye of writing is chieflye (yf wee respect oure old latin Poëtes) too bee affurded too *Virgil* in this wurck, and too *Ouid* in his *Metamorphosis*. As for *Ennius, Horace, Iuuenal, Persius* and thee rablement of such cheate Poëtes, theyre dooinges are, for fauoure of antiquitye, rather

to be pacientlye allowed, thean highlye regarded. Such
leauinges as wee haue of *Ennius* his ragged verses are
nothing current, but sauoure soomwhat nappy of thee
spigget, as one that was neauer accustomed too strike vp
thee drum, and too crye, in blazing martial exploytes,
alarme, but when hee were haulfe tipsye, ac *Horace* recordeth.
Thee oother three, ouer this that theyre Verses in camfering
wise run harshe and rough, perfourme nothing in matter, but
biting quippes, taunting Darcklye certeyn men of state, that
liued in theyre age, beesprinckling theyre *inuectiues* with soom
moral preceptes, aunswerable too thee capacitye of eurie weake
brayne. But oure *Virgil* not content wyth such meigre stuffe,
dooth laboure, in telling, as yt were a *Cantorburye tale*, too
ferret owt thee secretes of *Nature*, with woordes so fitlye
coucht, wyth verses so smoothlye slyckte, with sentences so
featlye orderd, with orations so neatlie burnisht, with
similitudes so aptly applyed, with eeche *decorum* so duely
obserued, as in truth hee hath in right purchased too hym
self thee name of a surpassing poët, thee fame of an od
oratoure, and thee admiration of a profound philosopher.
Hauing therefore (mi good lord) taken vpon mee too execute
soom part of master *Askam* his wyl, who, in his goulden
pamphlet, intituled *thee Schoolemayster*, dooth wish thee
Vniuersitie students too applie theyre wittes in bewtifying
oure English language with heroical verses: I heeld no
Latinist so fit, too geeue thee onset on, as *Virgil*, who, for
his peerelesse style, and machlesse stuffe, dooth beare thee
prick and price among al thee Roman Poëts. How beyt I
haue heere haulf a guesh, that two sortes of carpers wyl
seeme too spurne at this myne entreprise. Thee one vtterlie
ignorant, thee oother meanelye letterd. Thee ignorant wyl
imagin, that thee passage was nothing craggye, in as much

as M. *Phaere* hath broken thee ice before mee : Thee meaner
clarcks wyl suppose, my trauail in theese heroical verses too
carrye no great difficultie, in that yt lay in my choise, too
make what word I would short or long, hauing no English
writer beefore mee in this kind of poëtrye with whose squire
I should leauel my syllables.   Too shape therefor an answer
too thee first, I say, they are altogeather in a wrong box :
considering that such woordes, as fit M. *Phaer*, may bee very
vnapt for mee, which they would confesse, yf theyre skil
were, so much as spare, in theese verses.   Further more I
stand so nicelie on my pantofles that way, as yf I could,
yeet I would not renne on thee skore with M. *Phaer*, or ennie
oother, by borrowing his termes in so copious and fluent a
language, as oure English tongue is.   And in good sooth
althogh thee gentleman hath translated *Virgil* intoo English
rythme with such surpassing excellencie, as a verie few (in
my conceit) for pyekt and loftie wordes can burd hym, none,
I am wel assured, ouergoe hym : yeet hee hath rather
dubled, than defalckt oght of my paines, by reason that in
conferring his translation with myne, I was forced, too weede
owt from my verses such choise woordes, as were forestald
by him : vnlesse they were so feeling, as oothers could not
countreuaile theyre signification : In which case yt were
no reason, too sequester my pen from theyre acquaintance,
considering, that as M. *Phaer* was not thee first founrder, so
hee may not bee accoumpted thee only owner of such termes.
Truely I am so far from embeazling his trauailes, as that for
·thee honoure of thee English, I durst vndertake, too renne
ouer theese bookes agayne, and too geeue theym a new
liuerie in such different wise, as they should not iet with
M. *Phaer* his badges, ne yeet bee clad with this apparaile,
wherewith at this present they coom furth atyred.   Which

I speake not of vanitie, too enhaunce my coonning, but of meere véritie, too aduaunce thee riches of oure speeche. More ouer in soom poinctes of greatest price, where thee matter, as yt were, doth bleede, I was mooued too shun M. *Phaer* his enterpretation, and clinge more neere too thee meaning of myne authoure, in slising thee husk and cracking thee shel, too bestow thee kernel vpon thee wyttye and enquisitiue reader. I could lay downe heere sundrye examples, were yt not I should bee thoght ouer curious, by prying owt a pimple in a bent : but a few shal suffice. In thee fourth booke, *Virgil* deciphering thee force of *Mercurye* among oother properties wryteth thus.

> *Dat somnos adimitque, et lumina morte resignat.*

M. *Phaer* dooth English yt in this wise.

> *And sleepes therewyth he geeues and takes, and men from death defendes.*

Myne enterpretation is this : [*p.* 103.]

> *Hee causeth sleeping and bars, by death cyclyd vphasping.*

This is cleene contrarie too M. *Phaer.* Hee wryteth, that *Mercurye* defendeth from *death*, I wryte that yt procureth *death*, which (vnder his correction) dooth more annere too the author his mynd, and too *natures* woorcking. For yf *Mercurye* dyd not slea beefore yt dyd salue, and procurd sleeping eare yt caused waking, *Nature* in her operations would bee founderd, thee fat were in thee fire, thee marcket were mard. Too lyke effect *Chauncer* bringeth, in thee fift booke, *Troilus* thus mourning.

> *Thee owle eeke, which that hight Ascaphylo,*
> *Hath after mee shright al theese nightes two :*
> *And God Mercurye, now of mee woful wreche*
> *Thee soule gyde, and when thee list, yt feche.*

Againe *Virgil* in diuerse places inuesteth *Juno* with this epitheton, *Saturnia*, M. *Phaer* ouerpasseth yt, as yf yt were an idle woord shuffled in by thee authoure too dam vp thee chappes of yawning verses. I neauer, too my remembraunce, omitted yt, as in deede a terme that carieth meate in his mouth, and so emphatical, as thee ouerslipping of yt were in effect thee chocking of thee poet his discourse, in suche hauking wise, ac yf hee were throtled with the chincoughe. And too inculcat that clause thee better, where thee marriadge is made in thee fourth booke beetweene *Dido* and *Æneas*, I ad in my verse, *Watrye Iuno*, Althogh mijne authour vsd not thee epitheton, *Watrye*, but only made mention of *earth*, *ayer*, and *fyere*: yeet I am wel assured, that woord throughly conceaued of an heedeful student may geeue hym such light, as may ease hym of six moonethes trauaile: which were wel spent, yf that *Wedlock* were wel vnderstood. Thus *Virgil* in his *Æneis*, and *Ouid* in his *Metamorphosis* are so tickle in soom places, as they rather craue a construction than a translation. But yt may bee heere after (yf God wil grace my proceedings) I shal bee occasioned, in my *Fin Couleidos*, too vnlace more, of theese mysteries. Which booke I must bee manye yeeres breedinge: but yf yt bee throughly effected, I stand in hoape, yt wyl fal owt too bee *gratum opus*, not *Agricolis*, but *Philosophis*.

Now too coom too theym, that guesh my trauaile too be easye, by reason of thee libertye I had in English woordes (for as I can not deuine vpon such bookes, that happlye rouke in studentes mewes, so I trust, I offer no man iniurie, yf I assume too my selfe thee maydenhed of al wurcks, that hath beene beefore this tyme, in print, too my knowlegde, diuulged in this kind of verse) I wil not greatly wrangle with theym therein: yeet this much they are too consider.

that as thee first applinyg of a woord may ease mee in thee first place, so perhaps, when I am occasioned too vse thee selfe same woord els where, I may bee as much hyndered, as at thee beginning I was furthred. For example. In thee first verse of *Virgil*, I mak, *season*, long in an oother place yt would steede mee percase more, yf I made yt short: and yeet I am now tyed too vse yt as long. So that the aduantage that way is not verie great. But as for thee general facilitiec, this much I dare warrant yoong beginners, that when they shal haue soom firme footing in this kind of Poetrie, which by a litle payneful exercise may bee purchast, they shal find as easye a veyne in thee English, as in thee Latin verses, yee and much more easye than in the *English rythmes*. Touching myne owne trial, this much I wil discoouer. Thee three first bokes I translated by startes, as my leasure and pleasure would serue mee. In thee fourth booke I did task my self, and persued thee matter soomwhat hoatlie. M. *Phaer* tooke too thee making of that booke fifteene dayes. I hudled vp myne in ten. Wherein I coouet no prayse, but rather doe craue pardon. Fore lyke as forelittring biches whelp blynd puppies, so I may bee perhaps entwighted of more haste then good speede, as *Syr Thomas More* in lyke case gybeth at one that made vaunt of certeyn pild verses clowted vp *extrumpere.*

Hos quid te scripsisse mones ex tempore versus ?
Nam liber hoc loquitur, te reticente, tuus.

But too leaue that too thee veredict of oothers (wherein I craue thee good lyking of thee curteouse, and skorne thee controlment of thee currish, as those that vsuallie reprehend moste, and yeet can amend leaste) thee ods beetweene *verses* and *rythme* is verye great. For in thee one euerye *foote,* euerye *word*, euerye *syllable,* yet euery *letter* is too bee

obserued: in thee oother thee last *woord* is onlye too bee
heeded: As is very liuelye exprest by thee *lawyer* in empaneling
a iurye.

Johannes Doa: *Iohannes Den:*   *Johannes Hye:*
Richardus Roa: *Willielmus Fen:*   *Thomas Pye:*   M. Kytchin in Courtleete.
Iohannes Myles: *Willielmus Neile:*   *Richardus Leake:*   pag. 51. A.
Thomas Giles: *Iohannes Sneile:*   *Johannes Peake.*

Happlye such curious *makers*, as youre lordship is, wyl
accompt this but *rythme dogrel*: but wee may suite yt wyth a
more ciuil woord, by terming yt, *rythme peale meale*, yt rowles
so roundlye in thee hyrer his eares. And are there not
diuerse skauingers of draftye poëtrye in this oure age, that
bast theyre papers with smearie larde sauoring al too
geather of thee frynig pan? What *Tom Towly* is so simple,
that wyl not attempt, too bee a *rithmoure?* Yf your Lordship
stand in doubt thereof, what thinck you of thee *thick skyn*,
that made this for a *fare wel* for this *mystresse* vpon his
departure from *Abingtowne?*

> *Abingtowne, Abingtowne God bee wyth thee:*
> *For thou haste a steeple lyke a dagger sheathe.*

And an oother in thee prayse not of a steeple, but of a
dagger.

> *When al is goane but thee black scabbard,*
> *Wel faer thee haft wyth thee duggeon dagger.*

Thee therd (for I wyl present your lordship with a leshe) in
thee commendacion of bacon.

> *Hee is not a king, that weareth satten,*
> *But hee is a king, that eateth bacon.*

Haue not theese men made a fayre speake? If they had put
in *Mightye Joue*, and *Gods* in thee plural number, and *Venus*

with *Cupide thee blynd Boy*, al had beene in thee nick, thee rythme had beene of a right stamp. For a few such stiches boch vp oure newe fashion makers. Prouyded not wyth-standing alwayes that *Artaxerxes*, al be yt hee bee spurgalde, beeing so much gallopt, bee placed in thee dedicatorye epistle receauing a cuppe of water of a swayne, or elles al is not wurth a beane. Good God what a frye of such *wooden rythmours* dooth swarme in stacioners shops, who neauer enstructed in any grammar schoole, not atayning too thee paringes of thee Latin or Greeke tongue, yeet lyke blynd bayards rush on forward, fostring theyre vayne conceites wyth such ouerweening silly follyes, as they reck not too bee condemned of thee learned for ignorant, so they bee com-mended of thee ignorant for learned. Thee reddyest way therefore too flap theese droanes from thee sweete senting hiues of *Poëtrye*, is for thee learned too applye theym selues wholye (yf they be delighted wyth that veyne) too thee true making of verses in such wise as thee *Greekes* and *Latins*, thee fathers of knowledge, haue doone; and too leaue too theese doltish coystrels theyre rude rythming and balduck-toom ballads. Too thee sturring therefor of thee riper, and thee encouraging of thee yonger gentlemen of oure *Vniuersityes* I haue taken soom paynes that way, which I thoght good too beetake too youre lordship his patronage, beeing of yt self oother wise so tender, as happly yt might scant endure thee typpe of a frumping phillippe. And thus omitting al oother *ceremonial complementoes* beetweene youre lordship and mee, I commit you and youre proceedinges too thee garding and guiding of thee almightie.

From *Leiden* in *Holland* thee last of Iune. 1 5 8 2.

Youre Lordship his loouing broother
Richard Stanyhurst.

N thee obseruation of quantitees of syllables, soom happlye wyl bee so stieflie tyed too thee ordinaunces of thee Latins, as what shal seeme too swarue from theyre maximes, they wyl not stick too skore vp for errours. In which resolution such curious *Priscianistes* dooe attribute greater prerogatiue too thee Latin tongue, than reason wyl affurd, and lesse libertye too oure language, than nature may permit. For in as much as thee Latins haue not beene authors of theese verses, but traced in thee steps of thee Greekes, why should we with thee stringes of thee Latin rules cramp oure tongue, more than the Latins doe fetter theyre speeche, as yt were, wy+h thee chaynes of thee greeke preceptes. Also that nature wyl not permit vs too fashion oure wordes in al poinctes correspondent too thee Latinistes may easely appeere in suche termes as we borrow of theym. For exemple : The first of, *Breuiter*, is short, thee first of, *briefly*, wyth vs must bee long. Lykewise, *sonans*, is short, yeet, *sowning*, in English must bee long: and much more yf yt were, *Sounding*, as thee ignorant generaly, but falslye dooe wryte ; nay, that where at I woonder more, thee learned trip theyre pennes at this stoane, in so much as M. *Phaer* in thee verye first verse of Virgil mistaketh thee woorde, Yeet *sound* and *sowne* differ as much in English, as *solidus* and *sonus* in Latin. Also in thee midest of a woord wee differ soomtymes from the Romans. As in Latin wee pronounce, *Orátor, Auditor, Magíster*, long : in English, *Orátoure, Auditoure, Magístrat*, short. Lykewise wee pro-

nounce, *Præpăro, compăro,* short in Latin, and *prepăred* and *compăred* long in English. Agayne thee infallibelist rule that thee Latins haue for thee quantitye of middle syllables is this. *Penultima acuta producitur, vt virtûtis; penultima grauata corripitur, vt sanguînis.* *Honoure* in English, is short, as with thee Latins: yeet *dishonour* must bee long by thee formoure maxime: which is contrary too an oother ground of thee Latins, whereby they prescribe, that thee *primatiue* and *deriuatiue* thee *simple* and *compound* bee of one quantitye. But that rule of al oothers must be abandoned from thee English, oother wise al woordes in effect should bee abridged. *Moother,* I make long. Yeet *graundmother* must bee short. *Buckler,* is long; yeet *swashbuckler* is short. And albeyt that woord bee long by *position,* yeet doubtlesse thee natural dialect of English wyl not allow of that rule in middle syllables, but yt must bee of force with vs excepted, where thee natural pronuntiation wyl so haue yt. For ootherwise wee should bannish a number of good and necessarye wordes from oure verses; as *M. Gabriel Haruye* (yf I mystake not thee gentleman his name) hath verye wel obserued in one of his familiar letters: where hee layeth downe diuerse wordes straying from thee Latin preceptes, as *Maiestye, Royaltye, Honestie,&c.* And soothly, too my seeming, yf thee coniunction, *And,* were made common in English, yt were not amisse, although yt bee long by *position:* For thee Romans are greatly aduantaged by theyre woordes, *Et, Que, Quoque, Atque:* which were they disioincted from thee Latin poëtrie, many good verses would bee rauelde and dismembred, that now cary a good grace among theym, hauing theyre ioynctes knit with theese copulatiue sinnewes. But too rip vp further thee peculiar propretye of oure English, let vs listen too *Tullye* his iudgement, wherein thogh hee seeme verie peremptorie, yeet, with his fauoure, hee misheth thee cushen. Thus in his booke, intituled *Orator,* hee writeth. *Ipsa natura, quasi*

*modularetur hominum orationem, in omni verbo posuit acutam
vocem, nec vna plus, nec a postrema syllaba citra tertiam.*   In
this saying Tullye obserueth three poinctes.   First, that by
course of *Nature* euerye woord hath an *accent*.   Next, one
only: lastlye, that thee sayd *accent* must be on thee last
syllable, as *propè*, or on thee last saluing one, as *Virtûtis*, or
at thee furthest on thee therd syllable, as *Omnipotens*.   Yeet
this rule taketh no such infallible effect with vs, althogh
Tully maketh yt natural, who by thee skyl of thee Greek
and Latin dyd ayme at oother languages too hym vnknowen,
and therefor is too bee borne wythal.   As, *Peremtorie*, is a
woord of foure syllables, and yeet thee *accent* is in thee first.
So *Sêcundarie, ôrdinarie, Mâtrimonie, Pâtrimonie, Plânetarie,
împeratiue, Côsmographie, ôrtography*, with many lyke.   For
althogh thee ignorant pronounce, *Jmpêratiue, Cosmôgraphie,
Ortôgraghy*, geeuing the *accent* too thee therd syllable, yeet that is
not thee true English pronuntiation.   Now put case thee cantel
of thee Latin verse (*Sapiens dominabitur astris*) were thus Eng-
lished : *Planetary woorckinges thee wismans vertue represseth :*
albeyt thee middle of *planeta* bee long with thee Romans, yeet
I would not make yt scrupulus, too shorten yt in English,
by reason thee natural pronountiation would haue yt so.   For
thee final eende of a verse is to please thee eare, which must
needes bee thee vmpyre of thee woord, and according too that
weight oure syllables must bee poysed.   Wherefor syth thee
poëtes theymselues aduouch, *Tu nihil inuita facies, discesue
Minerua.*   That nothing may bee doone or spoaken agaynst
nature, and that *Art* is also bound too shape yt self by al
imitation too *Nature*: wee must request theese *grammatical
Precisians*, that as euery countrye hath his peculiar law,
so they permit euerye language too vse his particular loare.
For my part I purpose not too beat on euerye childish tittle,
that concerneth *Prosodia*, neither dooe I vndertake too chalck
owt any lines or rules too others, but too lay downe too thee

reader his view thee course I tooke in this my trauaile. Such woordes as proceede from thee Latin, and bee not altred by oure English, in theym I obserue thee quantitie of thee Latin. As *Honest, Honor:* a few I excepted, as thee first of *apeered, auenture, aproched,* I make short, althogh they are long in Latin: as *Apparco, Aduenio, Appropinquo:* for which and percase a few such woordes I must craue pardon of thee curteous reader. For ootherwise yt were lyke ynough that soom *grammatical pullet,* hacht in *Dispater* his sachel, would stand clocking aganyst mee, as thogh hee had found an horse nest, in laynig that downe for a falt, that perhaps I cooe knowe better then hee. Yeet in theese *diriuations* of termes I would not bee doomde by euerye reaching herrault, that in roaming wise wyl attempt too fetche thee petit degree of woordes, I know not from what auncetoure. As I make thee first of *Riuer* short. A Wrangler may imagin yt should bee long, by reason of *Riuus,* of which yt seemeth too bee deriued. And yeet forsooth *riuus* is but a *brooke,* and not a *riuer.* Likewyse soom English woordes may bee read in soom places long, in soom short, as *skyeward, seaward, scarowme.* Thee difference thereof groweth beecause they are but compound woordes that may bee with good sense sunderd: and thee last of *Sea,* and *skye* beenig common breedeth that diuersitie. Also thee self same woord may varye beecause of thee signification. Thee first of *Felon* for a *theefe* I make long, but when yt signifieth thee disease, so named, I hold yt better too make yt short. Agayne a woord that is short beeing deuided, may bee long in an oother place contracted. As thee first of, *Leaues,* yf you deuide yt in two syllables, I make short, yf you contract yt too one syllabe I make yt long. So thee first in *Crauing* is long, and thee therd person of thee verb, too wyt, *Craues,* may seeme short, where the next woord following beginneth with a vocal, yet yt is long by contraction: and so diuerse lyke woordes are too bee taken. And truely such nice obseruations that *Grammarians* dooe prescribe are not by thee choysest poëtes alvvayes so preciselye put in execution: as in this oure authour I haue by thee vvay marckt. In thee fore front of thee first booke hee maketh thee first of *Lauinum* long. In thee same booke hee vseth yt for short. Likevvise dooth he varie thee first of *Sichæus*. So in thee therd booke thee midest of *Cyclopes* soomtyme is made long, soomtyme short. And in the same booke the coniunction, *Que*, is long. As

> *Liminaque laurusque Dei totusque moueri.*

And in thee fourth:

> *Cretésque Driopesque ferunt, pictique Agathyrsi:*

Also thee first of *Jtalia* is long: yeet in thee therd book *Jtalus* is short: as:

> *Has autem terras, Italique hanc littoris oram.*

Touching the *termination* of syllables, I made a *prosodia* too my selfe squaring soomvvhat from thee Latin: in this vvise.

A finita communia.

B. D. T. Breuia: yeet theese vvoordes that eende lyke dipthonges are common: as *mouth, south, &c.*

C common.

E common: yf yt bee short, I vvryte yt vsualy vvith a single E. as *the, me.* yf long vvith tvvo, as *thee, mee.* althogh I vvould not vvish thee quantitie of syllables too depend so much vpon thee gaze of thee eye, as thee censure of thee eare.

F. breuia.

G. breuia: soomtyme long by *position* vvhere D may bee enterserted, as *passage* is short, but yf you make yt long, *passadge* vvith, D. vvould bee vvritten, albeyt, as I sayd right novv, thee eare not ortographie must decyde thee quantitye, as neere as is possible.

I. common.

K. common.

L. breuia, præter Hebræa, vt *Michaël, Gabriel.*

N. Breuia, yeet vvoordes eending in dipthongvvise vvould bee common, as *playne, fayne, swayne.*

O. common, præter ô longum.

P. Breuia.

R. Breuia. except vvoordes eending lyke dipthonges that may bee common, as *youre, oure, houre, soure, succour, &c.*

As and Es common.

Is breuia.

Os common.

Vs breuia.

V. common.

As for M. yt is either long by *position,* or els clipt, yf thee next vvoord begyn vvith a vocal: as *fame, name:* for albeyt. E. bee thee last letter, that must not salue. M. from accurtation, beecause in thee eare M. is thee last letter, and E dooth noght els but leng[t]hen and mollifye thee pronountiation.

As for. I. Y. VV. in as much as they are moungrels, soomtyme consonantes, soomtyme vocals, vvhere they further I dooe not reiect theym, vvhere they hinder, I doe not greatlye vveigh theym. As thee middle of *folowing* I make short, notvvythstanding thee VV: and lykvvise the first of *power.* But vvhere a consonant immediatly follovveth the VV, I make yt alvvayes long as *fowling.*

This much I thoght good too acquaynt thee gentle reader vvythal, rather too discoouer, vvyth vvhat priuat preceptes I haue embayed my verses, then too publish a *directorye* too thee learned vvho in theyre trauayls may franckly vse theyre ovvne discretion, vvythovvt my direction.

THE FIRST BOO-
KE OF VIRGIL
HIS ÆNEIS.

 That in old season wyth reeds oten harmonye
  whistled
My rural sonnet; from forrest flitted (I) forced
Thee sulcking swincker thee soyle, thoghe
  craggie, to sunder.
A labor and a trauaile too plowswayns hertelye
  welcoom.
Now manhod and garbroyls I chaunt, and martial horror.
I blaze thee captayne first from Troy cittye repairing,
Lyke wandring pilgrim too famosed Italie trudging,
And coast of Lauyn : soust wyth tempestuus hurlwynd,
On land and sayling, bi Gods predestinat order :
But chiefe through Iunoes long fostred deadlye reuengment.
Martyred in battayls, ere towne could statelye be buylded,
Or Gods theare setled : thence flitted thee Latin ofspring,
Thee roote of old Alban: thence was Rome pecreles
  inhaunced.
  My muse shew the reason, what grudge or what furye
  kendled
Of Gods thee Princesse, through so cursd mischeuus hatred,
Wyth sharp sundrye perils too tugge so famus a captayne.
Such festred rancoure doo Sayncts celestial harbour ?
  A long buylt citty theare stood, Carthago so named,
From the mouth of Tybris, from land eke of Italye seauerd,

Possest wyth Tyrians, in streingh and ritches abounding.
Theare Iuno, thee Princes her Empyre wholye reposed,
Her Samos owtcasting, heere shee dyd her armonye settle,
And warlick chariots, heere chiefly her ioylitye raigned.
This towne shee labored too make thee gorgeus empresse,
Of towns and regions, her drift yf destenye furthred.
But this her hole meaning a southsayd mysterie letted
That from thee Troians should branch a lineal ofspring,
Which would thee Tyrian turrets quite batter a sunder,
And Libye land likewise wyth warlick victorye conquoure.
Thus loa bye continuance thee naues of fortun ar altred.
This Iuno fearing, and old broyls bluddye recounting,
Vsd by her Greeke fauorits, that Troian cittye repressed,
Her rancour canckred shee can not let to remember,
And Paris his scorning iudgement dooth burne in her
    entrayls.
Shee pouts, that Ganymed by Ioue too skitop is hoysed.
Shee bears that kinred, that sept vnmerciful hatred.
Wyth theese coals kendled shee soght al possibil engins
In surging billows too touze thee coompanie Troian.
Al the frushe and leauings of Greeks, of wrathful Achilles.
Through this wyde roaming thee Troians Italy mishing
Ful manye yeers wandred, stil crost with destenye backward.
Such trauail in planting thee Romans auncetrye claymed.
    Tward Sicil Isle scantly thee Troian nauye dyd enter,
And the sea salte foaming wyth braue flantadoe dyd harrow,
When that Iuno Godesse thee fuid most deadlye reuoluing
Thus to her self mumbled : shal I leaue my purpose
    vnaunswerd ?
Or shal I this Troian too seize thus on Italye suffer ?
Forsoth I stand letted by fats : and clarcklye recounted.
As thogh that Pallas could not bee fullye reuenged,
Thee Greekfleete scorching, thee Greekish coompanye
    drowning :
And for on his faulty practise, for madnes of Aiax ?
This Queene wyld lightninges from clowds of Iuppiter hurling

Downe swasht theyre nauy, thee swelling surges vphaling.
Thee pacient panting shee thumpt and launst wyth a
    fyrebolt,
And wythal his carcasse on rockish pinnacle hanged.
And shal I then Iuno, of Saincts al thee Princes abyding,
Both the wife and sister too peerelesse Iuppiter holden,
In so great a season wyth one od pild countrey be warring ?
If this geare cotten, what wight wyl yeelde to myn aulters
Bright honor and Sacrifice, wyth rits my person adoring ?
Thus she frying fretted, thus deepely plunged in anger
Æolian kingdoom shee raught, where blusterus huzing
Of wynds in Prison thee great king Æolus hampreth.
Theese flaws theyre cabbans wyth stur snar iarrye doe
    ransack,
Greedelye desyring too rang : king Æolus, highly
In castel setled, theyre strief dooth pacifie wisely.
But for this managing, a great hurly burlye the wyndblasts
Would keepe on al mayneseas and lands wyth woonderus
    humbling.
Thee father almighty this mischiefe warelye doubting
Mewed vp theese reuelers coupt in strong dungeon hillish,
And a king he placed, throgh whose Maiestical Empyre
Theese blasts rouze forward, or back by his regal
    apoinctment.
Too this princelye regent her suit ladie Iuno thus opned.
    Æolus (in so much as of mankind the Emperor heaunlye
And father of thee Gods too thee the auctoritye signed
Too swage seas surging, or raise by blusterus hùffling)
Thee water of Tyrrhen my foes wyth nauye doe trauerse :
Troy towne wyth tamd gods too land ek of Italy bringing.
Yeeld to the wynds passadge, duck downe theire fleete with
    a tempest,
Or ships wyde scatter, wyth fluds that coompanye swallow.
Nymphs do I keepe fourteene for peerelesse bewtye renowmed,
Of theese thee paragon, for fayrenesse, Deiopeia
To the in fast wedlock wyl I knit, thye wife onlye remayning

Thy pheere most faythful through eendles season abyding,
Thee father of fayre brats, for this thy curtesye, making.
  This labor is needelesse (deere Queene) king Æolus
    aunsward.
Thy mynd to accomplish my bounden duitye requireth.
For my mace and kingdoom through thy fast freendship I
    gayned.
Through thy freendlye trauaile mee dooth king Iuppiter algats
Tender : by thye labour wyth Gods at bancket I solace.
Thow madst me in tempest and blusturs loftelye ruling.
This sayd : with poyncted flatchet thee mountan he broached
Rush do the winds forward through perst chinck narrolye
    whizling ;
Thee land turmoyling with blast and terribil huzing.
They skud too the seaward, from deepe profunditie raking
Too the skye thee surges, the east west contrarie doe struggle
And southwind ruffling : on coast thee chauft flud is hurled.
Crash do the rent tacklings ; thee men raise an horribil
    owtcrye.
Thee clowds snach gloomming from sight of Coompanie
    Troian
Both Light and welken : thee night dooth shaddo the
    passadge.
Thee skyes doo thunder, thee lightnings riflye doe flush flash,
Noght breeds theym coomfort, eeche thing mortalitye
    threatneth.
Æneas (his lyms wyth sharp cold chillye benummed)
Dooth groane, then to skyward his claspt hands heauelye
    lifting,
Thus spake : O Troians, ô thrise most nobil or happye
That before eune the parents wyth byckring martial ended
Your liues at townewals : of Greekes ô woorthye the
    strongest
Stout Diomed : byethe filds of Troy what fortun vnhappye
Mee fenst from falling wyth thy fierce slaughterus
    handstroke.

Wheare lyes strong Hector slaughtred by manful Achilles.
Wheare stout Serpedon dooth rest, where gauntlet or
    helmet
In water of Simois, wyth souldours carcases harboure.
This kyrye sad solfing, thee northen bluster aproching
Thee sayls tears tag rag, to the sky thee waues vphoysing.
The oars are cleene splintred, the helme is from ruther
    vnhafted
Theire ships too larboord doo nod, seas monsterus haunt
    theym.
In typs of billows soom ships wyth danger ar hanging.
Soom synck too bottoms, sulcking thee surges asunder:
Thee sands are mounted: thee southwynd merciles eager
Three gallant vessels on rocks gnawne craggye reposed,
(Theese rancks the Italian dwellers doo nominat altars)
Lykewise three vessels the east blast ful mightelye whelmed
In sands quick souping (a sight to be deepelye bewayled)
One ship that Lycius dyd shrowd with faythful Orontes
In sight of captayne was swasht wyth a roysterus heape-
    flud.
Downe the pilot tumbleth wyth plash round soommoned
    headlong.
Thrise the grauel thumping in whirkpoole plunged is
    hooueld.
Soom wights vpfloating on raisd sea wyth armor apeered.
In foame froth picturs, wyth Troian treasur, ar vpborne.
Also wher Ilionus was shipt, where manful Achates
And what vessel Abas possest and aged Alethes
Were bulcht by billows and boarde by forcibil entrye:
Thee storme dyd conquoure, thee ships scant weaklye
    resisted.
    These vnrulye reuels, and rif rafs wholye disordred,
As broyl vnexpected, thee sea king Neptun awaked.
Sturd wyth theese motions, his pleasing pallet vpheauing
Hee noted Æneas his touzdtost nauye to wander,
And sees thee Troians wyth seas and rayne water heaped,

This spightful pageaunt of his owne syb Iuno remembring,
Thee wynds hee summond : and wroth woords statelye thus
vsed.
What syrs ? your boldnesse dooth your gentilitie warrant ?
Dare ye loa, curst baretours, in this my Segnorie regal,
Too raise such raks iaks on seas, and danger vnorderd ?
Wel syrs : but tempest I wyl first pacifie raging.
Bee sure, this practise wil I nick in a freendlye memento.
Pack hence doggye rakhels, tel your king, from me, this
errand.
Of seas thee managing was neauer alotted his empire.
That charge mee toucheth ; but he maystreth monsterus
hildens,
Youre kennels, good syrs : let your king Æolus hautye
Execut his ruling in your deepe dungeon hardlye.
Thus sayd, at a twinckling thee swelling surges he calmed
Thee clowds hee scatterd, and cleere beams sunnye recalled.
Cymothöe and Triton on steepe rock setled ar haling
Thee ships from danger : with forck king Neptun is ayding.
Hee balcks thee quicksands, and fluds dooth mollefye sweetly,
He glyds on the seafroth, with wheales of gould wagon,
easye.
In mydst of the pepil much lyke to a mutenye raysed
Where barcks lyke bandogs thee raskal multitud angry,
Now stoans and fyrebrands flundge owt, furye weapon
awardeth :
In this blooddye riot they soom grauet haplye beholding
Of geason pietce, doo throng and greedelye listen.
Hee tames with sugred speeches theyre boysterus anger.
In lykewise Neptun thee God, no sooner apeered
In coche : when billows theire swelling ranckor abated.
Thee weather hackt Troians to the next shoare speedely
posting
On Libye coast lighted : where they theire nauye reposed.
Theare stands far stretching a nouke vplandish : an Island
Theare scat, with crabknob skrude stoans hath framed an hauen.

This creeke with running passadge thee channel inhaunteth.
Heere doe lye wyde scatterd and theare cliues loftelye
    streaming,
And a brace of menacing ragd rocks skymounted abydeth.
Vnder hauing cabbans, where seas doo flitter in arches.
With woods and thickets close coucht they be clothed al
    vpward.
A cel or a cabban by nature formed, is vnder,
Freshe bubling fountayns and stoanseats carued ar inward :
Of Nymphes thee Nunry, wheere sea tost nauye remayning
Needs not too grapple thee sands with flooke of an anchor.
Hither hath Æneas with seaun ships gladlye repayred.
On sands from vessels dooth skippe thee coompanye
    cheereful,
Pruning theyre bodyees, that seas erst terribil harmed.
First on flint smiting soom sparcklinges sprinckled Achates,
In spunck or tinder thee quick fyre he kindly receaued.
With sprigs dry wythered thee flame was noourished aptly.
Foorth do they lay vittayls, with storme disseasoned heauy.
Theyre corne in quernstoans thye doe grind and toste yt on
    embers
In the while Æneas too rock crept loftye, beholding
In the sea far stretching yf that knight Antheus haplye,
Were frusht, or remanent of Troian nauye wer hulling :
Or Capis, or the armours high picht of manlye Caicus.
No ships thence he scried, but three stags sturdye wer vnder
Neere the seacost gating, theym slot thee clusterus heerdflock
In greene frith browsing : stil he stands and snatcheth his
    arrows
And bowbent sharply, from kind and faythful Achates :
Chiefe stags vpbearing croches high from the antlier hauted
On trees stronglye fraying, with shaft hee stabd to the
    noombles
Throgh fels and trenches thee chase thee coompanye tracked,
Theyre blades they brandisht, and keene prages goared in
    entrayls

Of stags seun migty; with ships thee number is eeuened.
With this good venery to the road thee captayn aproched
And to his companions thee kild stags equalye sorted.
With wyne theire venison was swyld, that Nobil Acestes
In shore Trinacrian bestowd with liberal offer.
Theese pipes Æneas then among thee coompany broched
And with theese speeches theyre myndes thus he cherrished
　　hautlye.
　O deere companions (for we erst haue tasted of hardnes)
Brawnd with woorse venturs, thee mightye God alsoe shal
　　eend this.
Through Sicil his raging wyld frets and rumbolo rustling
On peeres you sayled, through Cyclops dangerus helcaue.
On with a fresh courradge, and bace thoghts fearful abandon.
Of peril escaped much shal thee vearye remembraunce
Tickle vs in telling : through such sharp changeable hazards
And doubtful dangers, oure course tward Italye bending,
We must rush forward : oure seat theare destenye pitcheth.
Theare must thee kingdoom with Troian fame be reuiued.
Stand ye to your tacklings : and wayt for prosperus eendings.
　Thus did he speake manly, with great cares heauely
　　loaden,
His grief deepe squatting hoap he yeelds with phisnomye
　　cheereful.
They doe plye theire commons, lyke quick and greedye re-
　　pastours
Thee stags vpbreaking they slit to the dulcet or inchepyn.
Soom doe slise owt collops on spits yeet quirilye trembling,
Soom doe set on caldrons, oothers doe kendel a bauen.
With food they summond theyre force : and coucht in a
　　meddow
Theyre panch with venison they franck and quaffye carous-
　　ing,
When famin had parted, the tabils eeke wholye remooued,
They theire lost feioes with long talck greedye requyred.
With feare good coomfort mingling : yf so haplye they liued,

Or that their liues thee tempest bitter had eended.
But chiefly Æneas dyd wayle for manful Orontes
And for knight Amicus, thee fats ek al heauye reuoluing
Of Lycus and of sturdye Gyan, with woorthye Cloanthus.
 Now the eende neere streched; from seat when Iuppiter heunly
Thee seas, thee regions and eeche place worldlye beholding,
On Lybye land lastly fixt his celestial eyesight.
And thus as he mused, with tears Venus heauye beblubberd
Prest foorth in presence, and whimpring framed her errand.
 O God most pusiaunt, whose mighty auctoritye lasting
Ruls gods, and mankind skeareth with thunderus humbling:
What syn hath Æneas, my brat, committed agaynst the?
What doe the poore Troians? who with fel boucherye slaghtred
For bending passadge to the promised Italye, therefor
No worldly corner can theym securitye warrant.
You to me ful promist, eare that yeers sundrye wer eended,
That Roman famely should spring from the auncetrye Troian,
By whom thee worldly coompas should wholye be ruled.
Wherefor (mightye father) what dooth thy phansye thus alter?
I tooke soom coomfort, when Troy was latelye repressed,
With futur hap coomming, past fortun vnhappye requiting.
And yeet theese wretched vagabunds hard destenye scourgeth
When shal (Prince pusiant) theese dangers dryrye be canceld?
Antenor was habil, from Grekish coompanye slincking,
Too passe through Greceland saulfly to Lyburnical empyre.
Also to thee fontayn welspring of woorthye Timauus.
Where through nyne channels with mountayns murmerus hurring
Rough the sea floas forward, thee land with snarnoise en-haunting
Heere notwithstanding this founder buylded a cittye,
That Padua is cleaped, too linnadge Troian alotted.

And arms of Troytowne bearing: there he saulflie doth
    harboure.
Wee that are of kinred too the, and hast shrind in Olympus,
Oure ships are whelmed through ons implacabil anger.
(A pitiful reckning) we ar touzed, and from Italye feazed.
Is this your daughters ritche dowry? her stablished empire?

   Thee prince of mankind, father of Gods, mirrelye simpring
Lyk when he thee tempest with cheereful phisnomye calmeth,
Bust his prittye parat prating, and mildlye thus aunswerd.

   Feare ye not (ô darling) on thy syde destenye runneth.
Thee Roman townewals thow shalt see loftelye raysed,
And thy sun Æneas his glittring glorye to luster.
This much I determyn, my mind no partye shal alter,
Thy child Æneas (for sith such care the doth anguish,
Thee fates close coouerd I wyl to the playnelye set open)
Thy sun, I say, valiant shal foster in Italy garboyls,
Strong and sturddye pepil with wars and victorye trampling.
Theare shal he buyld cittyes, and theare lawes ciuil enacting,
Vntyl three summars shal coompas his hudge Lauyn em-
    pyre:
And, the Rutils conquourd, three wynters stormye be
    glyding.
But thy sun Ascanius, which is eeke surnamed Iulus,
(Ilus he was termed, whilst stood the great Ilian empyre)
Hee shal bee the regent, vntil yeers thirtye be flitted,
From the Lauin kingdoom the state and thee chiefty remoou-
    ing:
And with thick bulwarck shal he fence thee rampired Alba.
Heere thre hundred wynters shal raigne knight Hector his
    ofspring,
By Mars fyrye fatherd twyns tyl the Queene Ilia gender;
Romulus in forrest of wulues dugge nurrished eager
Shal take thee regiment, and towne wals statelye shal vpraise
Of Rome, thee Romans of his owne name, Romulus, highting.
This rule thus fixed no tyme shal limit, or hazard:
Endles I do graunt yt: nay further Iuno fel harted,

Thee seas, thee regions, thee skies so spightfulye moyling,
Shal cut of al quarrels, and with mee newlye shal enter
In leage with Romans, and gownesept charelye tender.
Theese thus ar establisht.   Theare shal cum a season her-
    after,
When thee sayd famely shal crush Greeks segnorye throughly.
Thee Troian Cæsar shal spire fro this auncetrye regal,
His rule too Garamants, too stars his glorye rebounding
Iulius of valerus princely surnamed Iulus.
Thow shalt hym settle, with his east spoyls fraighted, in
    heunseat,
Whom with relligious good vows shal magnifye diuerse.
Thee world shal be quiet, then shal broyls bluddye be finnisht.
Then playne sound dealing with laws of woorthye Quirinus
And Remus, his broother, thee Roman cittye shal order.
Thee gates of warfare wyl then bee mannacled hardly
With steele bunch chayne knob, clingd, knurd, and narrolye
    lincked.
Heere within al storming shal Mars bee setled on armoure
With brasse knots hundred crumpled ; with sweld furor
    haggish
Lyke bandog grinning, with gnash tusk greedelye snarring.
  Thus sayd : he foorth posted (by May borne) Mercurye
    downeward
That new buylt Carthage should house thee Troian asemblye.
Hee flitters swiftly with wynges ful fledgye beplumed
On Libye land seizing: ther he soone perfourmeth his er-
    raund.
Thee Moors are sweetned by Gods forwarned apoinctement,
But chief of al Dido, thee Queene, was wroght to the Troians.
  But the good Æneas in night with care great awaked
With Phœbus rising vpgot, too ferret al vncooth
Nouks of strang country, in what coast his nauye doth
    harboure ?
If men, or yf sauadge wyld beastes ther in onlye doe pasture.
For ther he no tillagde dyd find : thus was he resolued.

And what he discoouerd, too tel to the coompanye flatly.
His ships hee kenneld neere forrest vnder an angle
Of rock deepe dented, shaded with thickleaued arbours.
Hee walcks on priuat with noane but faythful Achates
Darts two foorth bringing with sharp steele forcibil headed.
In the myd of forrest as he gads, his moother aprocheth,
In weed eke in visage lyke a Spartan virgin in armour
Or lyke to Herpalicee, sweeft Queene, steeds strong ouer-
    ambling,
Which doth in her running surpas thee swift flud of Hebrus.
Shee bare on her shoulders her bow bent aptlye lyke huntresse ;
Downe to the wynd tracing trayld her discheaueled hearlocks ;
Tuckt to the knee naked : thus first shee forged her errand.
Ho syrs, perceaud you soom mayden coompany stragling,
Of my deere sisters with quiuer closelye begyrded
Rearing with shoutcry soom boare, soom sanglier oughly ?
So Venus: and to Venus thee soon thus turned his aunswer.
    We hard of no showting, too sight no sister apered.
    to the, fayre Virgin, what terme may rightlye be fitted ?
Thy tongue, thy visadge no mortal frayltye resembleth.
Thart, No doubt, a Goddesse, too Phœbus sister, or arcted
Too Nymphs in kynred : to the lasting glorye be graunted.
Smooth this craggye trauayl : tel what celestial harbour
Coompaseth our persons : theese men, this countrye we
    know not.
Vs to this od corner thee wynd tempestuus hurled.
This fist shal sacrifice great flocks on thy sacred altars.
    Then Venus: I daigne not my self wurth sutch honor heunly.
Of Tyrian virgins too weare thus a quiuer is vsed.
And to go thus thynly with wrapt vp purpil atyred.
Thow seest large Affrick, thee Moores, and Towne of Agenor,
Thee Libye land marckmears: a country manful in armoure.
In this coast Dido, from her broother flitted, is empresse.
Tedius in telling and long were the iniurye total :
Chief poyncts I purpose too touche with summarye shortnesse.
Her spouse Sichæus was namd, too no man vnequal

In lands, her dandling with feruent passion hoatly.
Her father in wedlock took to hym this virgin vnharmed.
But then her owne broother was by right setled in empyre,
Pygmalion named ; thee sinck and puddil of hateful
And furiouse cutthrots : hee murthred selly Sichæus,
With gould looue blynded iump at thee consecrat altars.
Of sisters freendsbip reckning; thee murther he whusted,
His syb in her mourning with long coynd forgerye feeding.
But loa, the proper image of corps vntumbed apeered
In dreame too Dido ; with pale wan phisnomye staring.
His brest he vncloased, thee wound, and bluddyful altars.
Thence to flit hee wild her, not long in countrye remayning,
Tward her costlye viadge his wief to hyd treasur he poincted,
Where the vnknowne ingots of gould and siluer abounded.
Dido so wel fornisht too flee with coompanye posteth.
Such folck as the tyrant pursude with vengeabil hatred,
Or feard his regiment in thronging cluster asembled.
They snach such vessels that then were rigd to be sayling
Pigmalions riches was shipt, that pinchepeny boucher.
And of this valiant attempt a woomman is authresse.
Theare they were enshoared, wheare thow shalt shortlye see
        townwals,
And citty vpsoaring of new Carthago to skytoppe.
Thee plat they purchast, that place first Byrsa they cleaped
And so much as a bulhyd could coompas craftelye getting.
But syrs, whence coom you ? what wights ? or too what
        abyding
Countrye do you purpose too passe ? Thee capteyn amazed,
And sobs deepe fetching, with sight ful sadlye thus aunswerd.
        O gay Godesse lustringe yf I made to the largelye recital,
Or that of oure troubles you would to the summarye listen,
Thee night thee sunbeams would shrowd in clasped Olympus.
Wee coom from Troytowne (of Troyseat yf haplye the rumoure
Youre ears hath tinckled) late a tempest boysterus haggard
Oure ships to Libye land with rough extremitye tilted.
I am kind Æneas, from foes thee snatcher of housgods

Stowd in my vessels : in skyes my glorye doth harboure.
Land I seek Italian : from loue my pettegrye buddeth.
I made from Troytowne with vessels twentye to seaward,
My dam myghtye Godesse gyding, I my destenye tracked.
Rackt with soure blustring seaun ships ar scantlye recoouerd
I lyke a poore pilgrim throgh desert angle of Affrick
Wander, thrust from Asian regions and fortunat Europ.
    Heere Venus embarring his tale thus sweetlye replyed.
What wight thwart, doubtlesse thee gods al greatlye doe tender
Thy state, neere Tyrian citty so lucklye to iumble.
Hence take thy passadge, to the Queenes court princelye be
    trudging.
Theare thy coompanions with battred nauye be landed,
With flaws crusht ruffling, with north blast canuased hurring.
Thus stand thy recknings, vnlesse me myn augurye fayleth.
Marck loa, se wel yoonder swans twelue in coompany
    flusshing
And the skytip percing, enchast with a murtherus eagel
Swift doe fle too landward, on ground al prest tobe seazed.
As theese birds feazed, theyre wyngs with iolitye flapping,
Sweepe the skye, with gladnes theyre creaking harmonye
    gagling,
Eunso thye companions, or now with saulftye be shoared,
Or, voyd of al danger, theyre ships are grappled at anchor.
Speedelye bee packing, keep on hardlye the playne beaten
    highway.
    This sayd shee turned with rose color heaunlye beglittred
Her locks lyke Nectar perfumes sweet melloe relinquisht.
Her trayne syd flagging lyke wyde spread Conopye trayled.
Her whisk shewd Deity, hee finding his moother, in anger
Chauffing ; thee fugitiue with theese woords sharplye
    reprooued.
    What do ye meane (moother) with an elf show, vaynelye
    thus often
Youre soon too iuggle ? why oure hands both claspe we not
    hardly ?

Why do we not playnely good speeches mutual vtter?
Tward citty trauayling thus he blames her forgerye masked.
But Venus enshrowds theym with a thick fog palpabil ayrye,
Vnseen of eeche person by sleight inuisibil armed :
Least soom theyre passadge with curius article hyndring
Would learne, whence they trauayld? Too what coast ar
    they repayring?
Shee to her loftye Paphos with gladnesse myrrye returneth :
Wheare stands her temple with an hundred consecrat altars ;
Smoaking with the encense; the loa pauement senteth of
    herbflowrs.
    In thee meane season they doe passe directlye to towne-
    ward
They trip too mountayns high typ, thee cittye but vnder
Marcking ; thee castels and turrets statelye beholding.
Æneas woondreth; where dorps and cottages earst stood,
For to se such sturring, such stuffe, such gorgeus handwoorck.
Thee Moors drudge roundly, soom wals are loftelye raysing ;
Soom mount high castels; soom stoans downe tumble al
    headlong ;
Soom mearefurth platforms, for buylding curius houses;
Soom dooe choose the Senat, sound laws and order enacting ;
Soom frame play theaters; soom deepelye dig harborus
    hauens ;
Soom for great palaces doo slise from quarrye the chapters.
Lyke bees in summar season, through rustical hamlets
That flirt in soonbeams, and toyle with mutterus humbling.
When they do foorth carry theyre yoong swarme fledggie to
    gathring :
Or cels ar farcing with dulce and delicat hoonnye :
Or porters burdens vnloads, or clustred in heerdswarme
Feaze away thee droane bees with sting, from maunger, or
    hiuecot,
Thee labor hoat sweltreth : thee combs tyme flowrye be
    sprinckleth.
    O wights most blessed, whose wals be thus happelye touring

Æneas vttred : thee towne top sharplye beholding.
Hee throngs in shryne clowd (a strang and meruelus order)
Through crowds of the pepil, not seene, nor marcked of
annye.
   In towns myd center theare sprouted a groauecrop, in
arbours
Greene weede thick shaded, wheare Moors from surge water
angry
Parted, a good token dyd find : for Iuno, the Princesse,
Theare the pate, in digging, of an horse intractabil vttred.
Thee wise diuined, by this prognosticat horshead,
That Moors wyde conquest should gayne with vittayl
abundant.
Heere to Iuno Godesse thee Princesse Dido dyd offer
A fayre buylt temple, with treasure ritchlye replennisht.
Thee stayrs brassye grises stately presented, here also
Thee beams with brazed copper were costlye bepounced.
And gates with the metal dooe creake in shrilbated harshing.
   In this greene frithcops a new sight newly repressed
Long feareful dangers : Æneas freshlye beginneth
For to raise his courradge : his sharp aduersitye treading,
For whilst in temple corners hee gogled his eyesight
Wayting for Dido ; the stat of thee cittye beholding,
Whilst craftmens coonning hee marckt with woonder amazed,
Hee spied on suddeyn thee conflicts Troian al ordred,
And that theire bickrings al soyls haue coompased earthly.
Hee seeth Atrides, Priamus, to both hurtful Achilles.
   Fast he stood : and trickling dyd speake : what nouke (syr
Achates)
In world what region do not our toyls liuelye remember ?
Loa the, se king Priamus ; soom crooms of glorye be resting.
Soom tears this monument and soom compassion asketh.
Pluck vp a good curradge ? this fame soom saulftye wyl
offer.
   Thus sayd, his hert throbbing with vayne dead pictur he
feedeth ;

Groane sighs deepe reaching with tears his lyers ful he
    blubbred.
Hee sees with baretours Troy wals inuironed hardly:
Heere Greeks swiftlye fleing, theym Troiyouths coompanye
    crushing.
Theare gad thee Troians: in coach runs helmed Achilles.
Hee weeps also, seing flags whit, with Rhesus his holding
In sleepe, whom napping, Tydides blooddye betrayed,
His fierce steeds leading to the camp, er al hungrye they
    grased
On Troian pasturs, or Xanth stream gredelye bibled.
Troilus hee marcked running, deuested of armour:
A lucklesse stripling, not a matche too coape with Achilles:
With steeds he is swinged, downe picht in his hudge wagon
    emptye,
Thee rayns yeet griping: his neck and locks fal a sweeping
Thee ground, his launce staffe thee dust top turuye doth
    harrow.
In thee meane season Troy dames too temple aproched
Of fretting Pallas, with locks vntressed al hanging,
With grief meeklye praying, with breast knocks humblye
    requesting.
Thee Godes hard louring to the ground her phisnomye
    drowped.
Theare thrise about Troywals with spight knight Hector
    is haled.
For gould his carcasse was sold by the broker Achilles.
Heere sighs and sobbing from brest vp he mightelye rooted,
Thus too see the wagon, thee spoyl, the vnfortunat ending
Of deere companion, thee lyke cars also doe sting hym,
For to se king Priamus, with his hands owtstretched,
    vnarmed.
Hymself hee marcked combyned with Greekish asemblye.
Hee noted Indye pepil, with swart black Memnon his armye.
Theare wear Amazonical woommen with targat, an haulf-
    moone

Lykning, conducted by frantick Penthesilêa,
No swarms or trouping horsmen can apale the virago,
Her dug with platted gould rybband girded about her.
A baratresse, daring with men, thogh a mayd, to be buckling.
  Whilst prince Æneas theese picturs woonderus heeded,
And eeche pane throghly with stedfast phisnomye marcked,
Too churche Queene Dido, thee pearle of bewtye, repayred:
Of liucly yoonckers with a galland coompanye garded.
In Cynthus forrest much lyke too swift flud of Eurot
Where Nymphs a thowsand do frisk with Princelye Diana.
On back her quiuer shee bears, and highlye the remnaunt
Of Nymphs surpassing with talright quantitye mounting.
Too se this, her spirit with secret gladnes aboundeth.
Such was Dido ioying, so she with regalitye passed,
With Princely presence thee wurcking coompanye cheering.
In the gate of the Godesse shee syts, neere temple his arches
In chayre stately throned, with clustring garrison armed.
Shee frams firmlye statuts, and task wurcks equalye parteth.
Or toyls too pioners by drawcut lotterye sorteth.
Now sees Æneas with a crowding sudden asemblye
Antheus and also Sergestus, doughtye Cloanthus,
And oother Troians with rough seas stormye besweltred,
Too soyl vnacquaynted by tempest horriblye pelted.
Hee stands astonyed, so woondreth lykwise Achates:
For to shakhands freendly fear bars, now gladnes on haleth.
But the case vnwytted theym lets, thearfor they resolued,
With darck clowd shaded, too learne theyr formor auentur,
Wheare ryde theyre vessels? why they coom? what caus is
      of hastning?
For they the pickt choisemen dyd cul from nauye, requesting
Mercye, to the temple trotting with meruelus houling.
When they wer in presence, of pleading pardon afurded,
Then the braue Ilionus thus stout deliured his errand.
  O Queene most pusiaunt, too whom king Iuppiter heunly
Too raise a new citty, by rare felicitye, graunted,
And to rule a countrey, with scepter of equitye, sturdy:

Wee caytiefe Troians, with storms ventositye mangled,
Doo craue thee (Princesse) from flams our nauye to guerdon.
Yeeld pytye, graunt mercy; flowrs of gentilitye pardon.
For we hither sayld not, thee Moors with an armye to
    vanquish;
Or from their region with prede too gather an heardflock.
Such valerus coorradge rarely men conquered haunteth.
Theare stands a region, by Greeke bards Hesperye named,
A wel known countrey, for strong and plentiful holden,
Theare dwelt th'Oenotrians; but in oure adge Italye
    cleaped,
So named of captayn : too this braue countrye we mynded
Too bend oure iourney.
But with a flaw suddeyn chauffing stormbringer Orion,
Spurnt vs too the waters: then sootherne swashruter huffling
Flundge vs on high shelueflats, to the rocks vs he buffeted
    after.
Heere then a poore remnaunt in this thy segnorye landed.
What fel beastlye pepil rest theer ? such barbarus vsadge
What soyle wyld fosters ? On sands they renounce vs an
    harboure.
They doe byd vs battayl, fro the shoare thee coompanye
    pushing.
If ye doe skorne mankind, and eeche wight mortal his
    harming,
Let Gods sharp Iustice in soom sort yeet be rememberd,
Oure king Æneas vs ruld, who for equitye rightful
Euerye man owtpassed, for feats and martial armoure.
'.f this prince matchlesse no mortal destenye daunted,
But yet is in breathing, from tempest saulflye recoouerd:
First begin a freendshippe, for he wyl make fullye requital.
In Sicil eek region fayre towneships sundrye be setled :
In that od Isle raigneth, from Troyblud spirted, Acestes.
Graunt foorth thy warrant in docks oure nauye too settle :
Graunt plancks from forrest too clowt oure battered inlecks ;
That we our king meeting may passe tward Italye sayling.

If Libye seas raging the liefe of this captayn haue eended,
If no good coomfort dooth rest of nobil Iulus:
Suffer vs at leastwise, with iagged nauye retyring
To Sicil oure passadge too bend, too famus Acestes.

    This speche had Ilionus: that song his coompanye chaunted.
Brieflye then heere Dido, with downe cast phisnomye, parled.
Rest ye quiet, Troians, your thoghts from danger abandon.
In great sundrye peryls, my state set rawlye me streineth
Too keepe thus the seacoast with ward and garrison heedeful.
Who doe not Æneas, or Troian cittye remember?
Theire valor and courradge, theyre fyrebrand glorius onsets?
Wee Moors, lyke dullards, are not so wytles abyding,
Nor Phebe from oure citty dooth so far sunder his horses.
Yf ye be determynd, too sayl to old Italye Saturne,
Or to Sicil backward to the king, right nobil, Acestes,
Ile ye man, esquipping youre ships with furniture aptlye.
Or wyl you soiourne in this my feminin empyre?
In towne you denisons I do make: let nauye be docked.
Troians and Tyrians I wyl with one equitye measure.
Would God your captayn with sootherne blastpuf inhurled
Heere made his arriual; but a watch tward mouth of eche
    hauen
Speedelye shal be placed, your chieftayn woorthye to ferret:
Wheather he through forrest dooth range, or wandreth in
    hamlets.

    This princelye promisse boldning both manful Achates
And father Æneas, thee clowd with greedines eager
Too cleaue they coouet: to Æneas thus first sayd Achates.

    Thow sun of heunlye Godesse, how stands thy phansye
    resolued?
Thow seest al cocksure, thy fleete, thy companye salued.
One ship is only absent, that in oure sight sanckt to the
    bottom.
Thy moothers prophecy to the remnaunt fitlye doth aunswere.
    Scant had he thus spoken, when clowd theym drossye
    relinquisht,

And from earthly thicknesse, too thinnesse vannished ayerye.
Theare stud vp Æneas, with glittring beautye redowning.
Godlyke in his feauture : for his heunly moother amended
His bush with trimming, his sight was yoouthlye bepurpled :
His looke sweete simpred, much lyke to the pullished iuerye
By crafts hand burnisht : or with Phœbe siluer enameld :
Or touch stoane brazed with deepe gould purelye refined.
Hee then vnexpected to the Queene thus brauelye replyed.
    Heere do I stand present, whom you so gladlye required,
Æneas Troian from stormes defalcked of Affrick.
Of trauayl of Troians, O Queene, thee succeres only.
Wee crooms of Troians with land and seafurye moyled,
Of welth dispoyled, lyke plodding stormebeaten haglers
From natiue country, from citty exiled abyding,
For theese thy benifits too make lyke freendlye requital
I may not, Dido : nay the routs of progenye Troian
Through wilde world scatterd, can not make woorthy
    repayment.
Thee Gods (yf Deitee worcks of wights godlye regardeth,
If right bee raigning, yf vertue is too be rewarded)
Yeeld to the lyke kyndnesse, What world, what vertuus
    heunly
Both father and moother gaue breath to so peereles a daughter.
Whilst hils cast shaddows, whilst streams to the seas be
    reuoluing,
Whilst stars ar twinckling in the orbs of fixed Olympus,
Thy fame with thine honor shal bee by eternitye blazed
To what coast I trauayl : Theese speeches duytiful vttred
Hee shaks Ilionus with right hand, alsoe Serestus
With lefthand, so doughtye Gian, so doughtye Cloanthus.
First was Queene Dido with a sight thus sudden apaled
Next with his hard venturs, and thus shee rendred her
    aunswer.
    Thou sun of hautye Godesse, what crooked dangerus
    hazards
Pursu thy person ? what seas thee terribil hither

Haue flounst ?   And art thow Æneas mightye, begotten
Of thy syre Anchises, and of Venus at Simo fountayne ?
I saw king Teucer whillon too Sidon aproching
Expulst fro his regions, his right with might too recouer,
And with ayd of Belus : then my sire Belus in Island
Of Cyprus raigned, that land with victorie maystring
From that tyme forward I knewe thee Troian auenturs,
Thee name of thee citty, what kings succeded in empyre.
Enne thee veri enimy thee Troians glorye did vtter.
And from theyre linnadge right hee deriued his ofspring.
Whearefor, freend Troians, with draw your selues to mye
    lodgings.
Mee the lyk hard venturs erst, and aduersitye suffring
In this new kingdoom good fortun lastlye reposed,
My self erst flighted to reliue thee flicted I learned.
    Thus shee discoursed : to palaice foorth statelye she leadeth
Thee prince Æneas ; when seruice godlye was eended.
Thee whilst to his nauy shee caused twentye fat oxen
Straight to be conueighed, with an hundred bristeled hudge-
    brawns,
Of sheepe lyke number with lambs : gods mightye rewarding.
But the inner lodgings were with regalitye trimmed.
In mydst of chaumber thee roume for bancket is apted,
Thee wals are cloathed with massy and purpuled arras,
Of plate great cupboords, thee gould embossed in anticque
Patterns, her linnadge by long fetcht pettegre trayling
Of syers thee bedrol with natiue countrye recorded.
Then the good Æneas (for carcking natural eggeth
Thee mynd of the parent) to the vessels posted Achates,
This to tel Ascanius, conducting hym to the cittye.
Thee syre in his darlings good successe chieflye reioyceth.
Lykwise he commaunded too bring from nauye the presents
Snacht from Troy ransackt, with gouldfrets ritchlye bedawbed.
Also the roabe pretiouse colored lyke saufred Achantus :
Which plad vested Helen, from Greece when to Troy she
    flitted ;

Her weeds of wedlock, that her haut dam Leda dyd offer,
Of price a rare present : also thee scepter he willed
Of the fayr Ilionee to be broght : this fayrye was eldest
Of Priamus daughters, this mace too carrye she woonted :
Thee pearle and gould crowns too bring with garganet heauye.
With this charge vttred to the vessels hastned Achates.

 But Venus in musing with caers intoxicat hudling
New sleights fresh forgeth : the face of trim prittye Cupido
Too chang with iuggling, whereby hee too Dido resorting
In place of Ascanius, with gyfts might carrye the Princesse
Too braynesick loouefits, to her boans fire smouldered huffling.
For Venus haulf doubteth thee Moors sly treacherus handling :
Iuno her tormenteth : by night this terror her haunteth.
This reason her sturring thus spake she to cocknye Cupido.

 My sweete choise bulcking, my force and my power onlye,
My baby despising thee bolts of Iuppiter angrye ;
Of the request I refuge, with meeke submission humbled.
Thou knowest Æneas, by broothers byrth to the lincked,
Through seas to haue wandred by Iunoes merciles hattred :
Thow knowst thee venturs : my grief thy hert often hath
  anguisht.
Dido enterteigneth this guest with curtesye ciuil.
Yeet do I stil feare me theese fayre Iunonical harbours.
In straw thear lurcketh soom pad : ycet wyl she be sturring.
Thearefor her endcwours with counter craftinis hynder.
Inflame thee Princesse with looues affection earnest
That mye sun Æneas with mee shee chieflye may dandle.
This drift too compasse let this my loare be wel heeded.
At the fathers sending thee boy to the cittye repayreth.
(Delicat Ascanius, whose forward succes I tender)
With many rich presents from Troyflams narrolye scaped.
This child fast sleeping wyl I lodge in loftye Cythêra,
Els on hil Idalium in seat sacred he shal be reposed.
Least that he this stratagem should find, or woorck wylye
  founder.
Thow shalt his visadge for a nights space fitlye resemble.

Thee gay boy kindlye playing, thee knowne lads phisnomye
    taking :
That when Queene Dido shal col the, and smacklye bebasse
    thee,
When quaffing wyncbols, when bancquets deyntye be serued,
When she shal embrace thee, when lyplicks sweetlye she
    fastneth ;
That then thow be suer, too plant thy poysoned hoatloeue.
   Too moothers counsayl thee fyrye Cupido doth harcken
Of puts he his feathers, fauoring with gatetrip Iulus.
But Venus enfuseth sweet sleepe to the partye resembled,
Too woods Idalian thee child nice cocknyed heauing
In seat of her boosom : neere senting delicat herbflowrs
Of pretious Maioram, with shade most temperat housed.
   But now thee changling with gyfts dooth trudge to the
    cyttye
On to the court posting : his gyde was trustful Achates.
When that he too chaumber, most stately decked, aproched
Dido sat on beadsteed with curtens gorgeus hanged.
Then father Æneas with Troian cluster asembled :
On palet of scarlet they were for cossherye setled.
Thee wayting seruaunts riche basons massye doe carrye
Alsoe wyping towels : maunchets sum in pantrye doe basket
Fiftye busy damsels with charge of buttrye be tangled
With flame eke relligiouse too fire the consecrat aultars.
Maydens, manseruaunts, of eche is there numbred an
    hundred,
That with princelye viand the tabils al francklye doe furnish.
Thee Tyrian lordings too Court most freshlye resorted.
On neeld wroght carpets theese guestes were al vsshered
    aptly.
Æneas presents they marck, they doe gaze at Iulus.
His face goodlye roset, with speaking forgerye feigned.
They doe look at mantel, with roabs of saffrod Acanthus :
To futur harme lotted : but chieflye the princes vnhappie
Is not with gazing contented fullye, but eauer

Shee doth eye thee presents: thee mopsy her phantasye
  lurcheth.
On father Æneas his neck thee dandiprat hangeth.
And to his great lyking his syre supposed he gayneth.
Heeskips too Dido : thee Queene with curtesye cheereful
Accepts thee princox: soomtyme she hym claspeth in armes.
Poore soule not wytting what great God her hoatlye besiegeth.
But this prittye peacock, his dames charge slilye remembring,
First of al attempteth too raze from phansye Sichæus.
With quick looue liuing fro the dead the affection haling :
Too new flamd liking her mynd, erst rustye, reducing.
When fare was finnisht the tabils eeke stately remooued
Hudge bols thick they placed, with garlands crownd the
  they mazars.
Al the palaice ringeth with stamp, a mutterus humming
Tinckleth through the entryes: the tapers eeke kendled ar
  hanging
From gold wyre glittring : thee night with brightnes is owted.
Heere thee Queene wylled that a massiue gould cup,
  abounding
With stoans coucht pretious, should bee presented ; her
  owne hands
Thee goulden goblet with spirt wyne nappye replennisht.
This cup king Belus with her old syers former al vsed.
Thee rout kept a silence, theese speeches Dido dyd vtter.
    Iuppiter (of guest folcks thee stay thwart truelye reported)
Graunt that this present Tyrian with Troian asemblye
May breede good fortune to our freends and kynred heer after.
Let make sport Bacchus, with good ladye Iuno, be present.
And ye, my freend Tyrians, thee Troian coompanye frollick.
    Thus sayd, with sipping in vessel nycelye she dipped.
Shee chargeth Bicias : at a blow hee lustelye swapping,
Thee wyne fresh spuming with a draught swild vp to the
  bottom.
Thee remnant lordings hym pledge: Then curled Iöppas
Twanged on his harp golden, what he whillon learned of Atlas.

How the moone is trauersd ; how planet soonnye reuolueth,
Hee chaunts : how mankind, how beasts dooe carrye their
    ofspring.
How floods be engendred, so how fire, celestial Arcture,
Thee rainebreede seunstars, with both the Trionical orders.
Why the sun at westward so tymely in wynter is housed.
And whye the night seasons in summer swiftlye be posting.
Thee Moors hands clapping, the Troians, *plaudite,* flapped.
    But with sundrye motiue demaunds Queene Dido the night
        space
Stretcht, then vnhappy being with looues sweet poyson
    atached,
Verye much of Priamus demaunding and much of Hector.
Also how thee darling of bright Aurora was armed ?
How Diameds horses were shapt ? how strong was Achilles ?
Nay guest, quoth the lady, decipher from the beginning
Thee Greekish falshood, with thy owne sharp venterus
    hazards.
For now seun summers ar spent, sence thy trauayl hardy
On land and sayling, lyk pilgrim, causd the to wander.

Finis libri primi.

THEE SECVND

BOOKE OF VIR-
GIL HIS ÆNEIS.

 Yth tentiue lystning eeche wight was setled
    in harckning,
Thus father Æneas chronicled from lofty
    bed hautye.
You me byd, O Princesse, too scarrify a
    festered old soare.
How that thee Troians wear prest by
Græcian armye.
Whose fatal misery my sight hath wytnesed heauye :
In which sharp byckring my self, as partye, remayned.
What ruter of Dolopans weare so cruel harted in harckning,
What curst Myrmidones, what karne of canckred Vlisses
That voyd of al weeping could eare so mortal an hazard ?
And now with moysture thee night from welken is hastning :
And stars too slumber dooe stur mens natural humours.
How be yt (Princelye Regent) yf that thy affection earnest
Thy mynd enflameth, too learne our fatal auentures,
Thee toyls of Troians, and last infortunat affray :
Thogh my queazy stomack that bluddye recital abhorreth,
And tears with trilling shal bayne my phisnomye deepelye :
Yeet thyn hoat affected desyre shal gayn the rehersal.
    Thee Greekish captayns with wars and destenye mated,
Fetching from Pallas soom wise celestial engyn,
Framd a steed of tymber, steaming lyk mounten in hudgnesse.

A vow for passadge they faynde, and Brute so reported.
In this od hudge ambry they ramd a number of hardye
Tough knights, thick farcing thee ribs with clustered armoure.
    In sight is Tenedos of Troy ; thee famosed Island ;
Whilst Priamus floorisht, a seat with ritches abounding.
But now for shipping a rough and dangerus harboure.
Theare lurckt theese minions in sort most secret abiding.
Al we then had deemed, to Græce that the armye retyred
Thearefor thee Troians theyre longborne sadnis abandon :
Thee gates vncloased they skud with a liuely vagare,
The tents of the enymyes marcking, and desolat hauen.
Heere foght thee Dolopans, theare stoutly encountred
    Achilles,
Heere rode thee nauye : theare battayls bluddye wear offred.
Soom do loke on dismal present of loftye Minerua.
Also they gaze woondring at the horse his meruelus hudg-
    nesse
And first exhorteth thee Troians seallye Tymetes
Too bring thee monument intoo thee cittye ; then after
For to place in stately castel thee monsterus Idol.
Wheather he ment treasons, or so stood destenye Troian.
But Capys and oothers diuing more deepelye to bottom,
Warelye suspecting in gyfts thee treacherye Greekish,
Dyd wish thee woodden monster weare drowned, or harbourd
In scorching fyrebrands : or ribs too spatter a sunder.
Thee wauering Commons in kym kam sectes ar haled.
    First then among oothers, with no smal coompanye garded
Laccoon storming from Princely castel is hastning,
And a far of beloing : what fond phantastical harebrayne
Madnes hath enchaunted your wits, you townsmen vn-
    happye ?
Weene you (blynd hodipecks) thee Greekish nauye retùrned ?
Or that theyre presents want craft ? Is subtil Vlisses
So soone for gotten ?   My lief for an haulf penye (Troians)
Either heer ar couching soom troups of Greekish asemblye,
Or to crush our bulwarcks this woorck is forged, al houses

For to prye surmounting thee towne : soom practis or oother
Heere lurcks of coonning : trust not this treacherus ensigne :
And for a ful reckning, I lyk not barrel or hearing.
Thee Greeks bestowing theyre presents Greekish I feare mee.
Thus sayd : he stout rested, with his chaapt staf speedelye
     running
Strong the steed he chargeth, thee planck rybs manfuly
     riuing.
Then the iade ; hit, shiuered, thee vauts haulf shrillye
     rebounded
With clush clash buzing, with droomming clattered humming.
Had Gods or fortun no such course destenye knedded :
Or that al our senses weare not so bluntlye benummed
Thear sleight and stratagems had beene discoouered easlye,
Now Troy with Priamus castel most statelye remayning.
     But loa, the mean season, with shouting clamorus hallow
Of Troytowne the shepheerds a yoncker mannacled haling
Present too Priamus : this guest ful slylye dyd offer
Hym self for captiue, thearby too coompas his heasting,
And Troian citty to his Greekish countrye men open.
A brasse bold merchaunt in causes dangerus hardye.
In doubtful matters thus stands hee flatlye resolued,
Or to cog : or certeyn for knauerye to purchas a Tyburne.
Thee Troian striplings crowding dooe cluster about hym :
Soom view thee captiue, soom frumping quillites vtter.
     Now lysten lordings, too Greekish coosinage harcken,
And of one od subtil stratagem, most treacherus handling
Conster al.
For when this princox in mydst of throng stood vnarmed,
Heedelye thee Troians marcking with phisnomye staring :
     Oh, quod he, what   region shal shrowd mee villenus
          owtcast ?
Whearto shal I take me forlorne vnfortunat hoaplost ?
From Greekish countrey do I stand quit bannished : also
Thee wrath hoat of Troians my blood now fierclye requireth.
     Thus with a sob sighing our mynds with mercye relenting

Greedelye we coouet, too learne his kinred, his errand,
His state, eke his meaning, his mynd, his fortun, his hazard.
Then the squyre emboldned dreadles thus coyned an aunswer.
    King: my faith I plight heere, to relate thee veritye
      soothlye.
I may not, I wyl not deny my Greecian ofspring.
Thogh Sinon a caytiefe by fortun scuruye be framed
A lyer hym neauer may she make, nor cogger vnhonest.
If that, king pusiaunt, ye haue herd earst haplye reported
Thee name of thee famouse Palamedes greatlye renowmed :
Thee Greeks this captayne with villenus iniurye murdred :
Hym they lying charged with treasons falslye, for hyndring
Forsooth theyre warfars : hym dead now dolfulye mourne
    they :
Too serue this woorthy, to hym neerely in kinred alyed,
My father vnwelthy mee sent, then a prittye page, hither.
Whilst he stood in kyngdoom cocksure, whilst counsel
    auayled,
Then we were of reckning ; our feats weare duelye regarded.
But when my coosen was snapt by wycked Vlisses,
(A storye far publisht, no gloasing fabil I twattle)
With choloricque fretting I dumpt, and ranckled in anguish:
My tongue not charming with fumimg fustian anger
Playnelye with owt cloaking, I vowd to be kindlye reuenged,
Eauer yf I backward too natiue countrye returned.
And thus with menacing lyp threats I purchased hatred.
Hence grew my crosbars, hence always after Vlisses
With new forgd treasons me, his foa, too terrefye coouets.
Oit he gaue owt rumours, hee fabled sundrye reportes,
Mee to trap in matters of state, with forgerye knauish.
His malice hee fostred, tyl that priest Calchas he gayned.
But loa, to what purpose do I chat such ianglerye trim trams?
What needs this lyngring ? syth Greeks ye hold equal in
    hatred,
Syth this eke herd, serueth ; speede furth your blooddye
    reuengement.

So ye may ful pleasure thee Greeks, and profit Vlisses.

Thee les he furth pratled, thee more wee longed in harcking,
Too learne al the reasons, no Greekish villenye doubting,
Thee rest chil shiuering he with hert deliuered hollow.

Thee Greeks theyre passadge very oft determined hom-
ward.
And clooyd with byckring theese wars they thoght to
relinquish.
Would God yt had falne so: yet yt had so truelye: but often
South wynds with wynter storming theyre iournye dyd hinder.
Also of late season, when the horse was finnished holye
Thee skyes lowd rumbled with ringing thunderus hurring.
With weather astonyed, with such storms geason agrysed,
Wee sent Euripilus too sacred Apollo for aunswer.
Too soon his this messadge ruful from the oracle vttred.
Thee wynds with bloodshed were swagd, with slaughter of
hallowd
Virgin, to Troy ward when first you bended a nauye,
Youre viage also hoamward a slaughter blooddye requyreth.
Thee wynd puffe blustring no blood but Greecian asketh.
When knight Euripilus this messadge crooked had opned,
Then we were al daunted, with trembling feareful atached,
What Greek for sacrafice thee God demaunded Apollo.
Shortlye the priest Calchas was broght by the shrewdwyt
Vlisses,
And now soar laboreth, too know what person is asked.
Diuerse dyd prophecy foorth with my destenye final.
That this new practise from my old foes treacherye
sprauleth.
Thee priest twise fiue dayes thee case with secreacye sealeth.
Hee maks it scrupulous forsooth with blooddye rehersal
Of tongue, too sacrifice a wight: hym pressed Vlisses
This not with standing, with long importunat vrging,
Of purpose Calchas mee wretch to the altar apoincted.
Thearto the rest yeelded; for what theym priuat had
anguisht,

On me they soone setled with publicque ioyful agreement.
With posting passadge thee day most dismal aproched,
Thee fruits al be ready, garland to mye temple is apted,
My scape I deny not, my flight from prison I knowledge,
Thee woas and the myry foule bogs for an harborye taking
Vntil they to seaward had packt, and sayles had hoysed.
Now shal I wayle, poore soule, from natiue countrye
　remoued,
Of father accoumpting my self, of chyldren al hoaplesse.
Whose giltlesse slaughter be my flight is lyke to be coompast.
Thee do I craue, Priamus, by Gods almightye supernal
(Yf truth, yf vnfayned good fayth dooth floorish among
　men)
For to spare a wretched fugitiue thus touzed in hatred.
Wee thawde with weeping doo pardon francklye the villeyn.
In person Priamus foorth with commaunded his yrons
For to be disioyncted, theese woords eke gratius adding.
　What wight th'wart, stranger, no Greekish countrye
　remember.
Thow shalt be a Troian ; yet in one doubt truelye resolue
　me.
What means this burly shapte horse ? what person is
　author ?
For what relligion ? what drift ? what martial engyn ?
　This sayd : my yooncker with Greekish treacherye lessond,
Too stars vp mounting both his hands vnmannacled,
　aunswerd.
　You fires perpetual with rits vnspotted abyding,
Too you for wytnesse do I cal : you mystical altars,
You swoords I fled from, that I woare, you consecrat
　headbands,
I do hold yt lawful, to reueale thee mysterye Greekish,
Too scorne theyre persons, to blab theyre secrecye priuat.
What law can bynd mee, to be trew to so wycked a countrey ?
So that you, Troians, in promist mercye be constant,
If truth I shal manifest, yf gifts bee largelye requited.

Thee Greeks assuraunce in Pallas whoalye remayned
And with her assistaunce theyre wars were shouldered always.
But syth Tydides, eke of euels thee founder Vlisses
Attempted lewdly fro the church to imbeazel an holy
Patterne of Pallas, thee keepers filthelye quelling,
Then they the sacred image with brude fist blooddye pro-
     phaned,
Thee virgins garlands with contempt impius handling :
Syth they that attempted, thee Greekish succes abated
And ther hoap al backward dyd drag : thee virgin eke angrye.
And her wrath the Godesse with signs most sensibil opned.
Scant was this patterne of Pallas setled among vs
When flams of firy flasshing most terribil hissed :
   It sweat with chauffing : three tymes (to to strang to be
      spoken)
From ground yt mounted, both launce and targat eke holding.
Through seas priest Calchas, to retyre back hastelye, wisheth
For that agaynst Troians thee Greeks doo vaynelye bear
     armoure.
Tyl that with the Godesse theymselues too Greece be returned.
Which they perfourmed. Now that they sayled ar hoame-
     ward
They puruey weapons and Gods too pacifye purpose,
And to returne hastly : thus Calchas eeche plat hath ordred.
They framd this monument to appease celestial anger
Of the Godesse Pallas, the prophet that practis apoincted.
Howbeyt, Priest Calchas would haue the horse lifted in
     hudgnesse,
Lest you, thee Troians, through gats should carrye the
     present.
And so to bee shielded yet agayn with patrónage anticque.
If you with violence this gyft too scatter had hapned,
Graund heaps of mischief (which Gods on the author his
     hertroote
First set (I doo pray theym) should Troian cittye replennish.
And yf this relliek by you to the cittye wer haled,

Then, loa, the stout Troians in wars should glorye triumphing,
Wee to ye, lyke bondslaues, our selues for vanquished offring.
   With this gay glosing of a stincking periured hangman
Wee wer al inucigled, with wringd tears nicetye blended.
Those whom Tydides, whom Lauissæan Achilles
And al theyre warlick vessels, in number a thowsand,
In ten yeers respit could not with victorye vanquish.
    But marck what foloed: what chaunce and luck cruel
      hapned
Iump with this cogging, our mynds and senses apaling.
As priest Laocoon by lot to Neptun apoyncted
A bul for sacrifice ful sizde dyd slaughter at altars,
Then, loa ye, from Tenedos through standing deepe flud apeased
(I shiuer in telling) two serpents monsterus ouglye
Plasht the water sulcking to the shoare moste hastelye
    swinging.
Whose brests vpstreaming, and manes blood speckled in-
    haunced
Hygh the sea surmounted, thee rest in smooth flud is hydden
Their tayls with croompled knot twisting swashlye they
    wrigled.
Thee water is rowsed, they doe frisk with flownse to the shoare
    ward,
Thee land with staring eyes bluddy and firie beholding:
Their fangs in lapping they stroak with brandished hoat tongs.
Al we fle from sacrifice with sight so grisled afrighted.
They charg Laocoon, but first they raght to the sucklings,
His two yong children with circle poysoned hooking.
Theym they doe chew, renting theyre members tender a
    sunder.
In vayne Laocoon the assault lyke a stickler apeasing
Is to sone embayed with wrapping girdle y coompast,
His midil embracing with wig wag circuled hooping,
His neck eke chayning with tayls, hym in quantitye topping,
Hee with his hands labored theyre knots too squise, but al
    hoaples

Hee striues : his temples with black swart poyson ar oyncted.
Hee freams, and skrawling to the skye brays terribil hoyseth.
Much lyke as a fat bul beloeth, that setled on altar
Half kild escapeth thee missing boucherus hatchet.
But theese blooddye dragons too sacred temple aproched
Vnder feete lurcking and shield of mightye Minerua.
A feare then general mens mated senses atached.
Wee iudge Laocoon to be iustly and woorthelye punnisht,
For that he rash charged with launce thee mystical idol.
Streight to place in citty this image, too pacifye swiftly
Thee Godes offended, they doe crye.
Downe we beat oure rampiers, our towne wals gapwyd ar
    opned.
Al we fal a woorcking, thee wheels wee prop with a number
Of beams and sliders, thee neck with cabil is hooped.
Through wals downe razed wee draw thee mischeuus engyn,
Ful bagd with weapons : sonnets are carroled hymnish
By lads and maydens, the roap ons to tip hertelye longing.
Hit slids, and menaceth futur hurt in cittye reposed.
ô Gods, ô countrey, ô Troywals stronglye be rampyerd
Foure tymes this monument at townegats staggred in entring,
Foure tymes with the armour close coucht thee paunch bely
    classhed.
How be yt, blynd bayards we plod on with phrensie bedusked,
And in thee castel we doe pitch this monster vnhappye.
By Gods commaundment thee trouth Cassandra reuealed,
Neauer in her prophecyes by the Troians seallye beleeued.
Wee for a last farewel doo deck through cittye the temples.
    Thee whilst night darcknesse right after soonset aproched,
With shaddowclowding earth, heun, and treacherie Greekish.
Thee Greeks that glyded through wals, al softlye be whusted.
Then the Phalanx Greekish dyd sayl with nauye wel ordred
From Tenedos : shinings of moone most freendlye doe gyde
    theym.
To the shoare acquaynted they doe shooue : fyre of admiral
    hoysed,

Streight Sinon, assured by Gods and destenye wrongful,
Thee stuf paunch closet from lincking ioynetlye releaseth.
Thee doores discloased, by roaps thee coompanye slided.
Tisandrus, Sthenelus captayns, hard herted Vlisses.
And Athamas, next also Thoas foorth ishued hastlye.
Also Neoptolemus, but of oothers chieflye Machäon.
Downe Menelaus is holpt, of the engyn forger Epëus.
Oure men ar assaulted, with sleepe, with druncknes asotted.
Thee watch they murthred, thee gats set eke open, a cluster
Of theyre companions they let in, thee coompanye lincketh.

    Then was yt a season, when slumber sweetlye betaketh
Eech mortal person by woont and natural order.
I, loa, then in sleeping, to my seeming sorroful Hector
Prest furth in presence, and salt tears dolfulye showred.
Harryed in steedyocks as of carst, black bluddye to visadge
With dust al powdred, with filthood dustye bedagled.
His feet ar vpswelling with raynes of bridil ybroached.
Woa me God, how greatly was he chaunged from that od
    Hector,
Too Troy that whillon dyd turne with spoyls of Achilles,
Or that with wyldfire thee Greekish nauye beskorched.
His herd was sloottish, thee blood, thick cluttred, his hears
    staynd.
Those wounds wyde bearing, that he neere thee cittye
    receaued :
I, then, as I deemed by myn own wyl, thearto not asked,
Wept, in this maner to hym speeches sorroful vttring.
    O star of al Troians, of towne thee prosperus holder,
What lets thee lingred ? from what far countrye, syr Hector,
Long loockt for coomst thow ? so that after dangerus hazards,
And diuers burials of freends, of kinred, of oothers
Wee tost now doe see thee.   By what chaunce filthye thy
    visadge
Is thus disfigured ? Theese wounds why mortal apeere they ?
    Hee litle accoumpted this fond and vanitye childish,
But sighs vpplucking from brest ful deepelye, thus aunswerd.

Thow soon of holye Godesse,from flame thy carcas abandon.
Thee foes haue conquerd, Troytowne is fired of al sydes.
Too citty and Priamus lief ynough Gods destenye graunted.
Yf that thee Troians hand stroaks could fortefye manful,
This fiste, Greeks hacking, that fensiue seruice had eended.
Too the recommendeth Troytowne theyr consecrat housgods.
Take theese for the pilots of fats, by theyr ayd seke a cittye.
Which stately townewals by thee shalstronglye be founded,
Through large seas passadge when thou shalt wander here-
after.
Thus sayd : thee garland, mee thoght, and Vesta the mightye
From altars down fetching, thee fiers eternal he quenched.
Thee whilst in citty there roard a changabil howling,
Stil the noise encreaseth (yea thogh that verye far inward
My father Anchises his court was setled in arbours)
Thee skrich rings mounting, increast is the horror of armoure.
From sleepe I broad waked, to top hastly of turret I posted.
And to the shril yerning with tentiue greedines harckned.
Much lyke as in corneshocks sindged with blasterus hurling
Of Southwynd whizeling : or when from mounten a rumbling
Flud raks vp foorrows, ripe corne, and tillage of oxen.
Downe tears yt wyndfals, and thick woods sturdelye tumbleth.
Thee crack rack crashing the vnwytting pastor amazeth.
Now Greeks most playnely their craft, long hammered,
opned.
Vulcan hath, in flaming, quit burnt, by his furnitur heating,
The house of Deiphobus, then next his neighbor his hous-
frame.
Vcalegon kendleth, Thee strand flams fyrye doe brighten.
Thee towns men roared, thee trump taratantara ratled.
Thus then I distracted, with al hastning, ran to mye weapons.
Too shock in coombats, or gard with coompanye castels
Mee my wyl on spurreth, thus wrath, thus phrensye me
byddeth.
And to dye with byckring I tooke for a glorius emprice.
But see : priest Panthus of towne and sacred Apollo

Panthus Otriades thee Greekish boucherye scaping,
Iſeeld in his hands holy rellicques, Gods conquered, also
His yoong prittye nephew, to the strandward speedelye trotting.
What news, syr Panthus? what forte were best to be
    fenced?
Scant sayd I theese speeches, when woords to me dolful he
    rendred.
Woorthye syr, our last houre is coom, too late to be mourned.
Wee were in old season Troians, Troy cittye was, also
Thee Troian glory floorisht : now Iuppiter hardned
Hath the state of Troians subuerted wholye. The pertlyke
Greeks thee flamd citty with ruthlesse victorye ransack.
Theire steed hath vpvomited from gorge a surfet of armdmen.
Fals Sinon aduaunced, with fire, consumeth al houses,
And flouts vs kindly : thee gats ar cramd with an armye.
Such troups as neauer too citty Troian aneered.
Soom stop al od corners, no nouke, no passage vnarmed.
They brandish weapons sharp edgde, to slaghter apoincted.
In first encounter thee watch to to weaklye resisted.
    With woords of Panthus, and with Gods herried order
Kendled, I run forward too rush throgh thicket of armoure,
Wheare shouts vpclymbing most rise, wheare is hertsad
    Erynnis.
Theare leags as feloes Ripheus strong, Iphitus hardy.
By moonshyne roaming Hispanis, so syr Dymas eager
Flanck furth oure vauntgard : next cooms thee lusty Chro-
    rœbus
Soon to Prince Mygdon, who then not lucklye repayred
Too Troy : with lyking of mad Cassandra bewitched :
Soon to king Priamus by law : thus he lawfather helping,
His pheers wood prophecyes not at al the yooncker vnhappye
Herd.
This band of Troians thus ioynctly assembled, I framed
This speeche : Stout gallants, braue youths, and coompanye
    manful,
Yf ye be determyned too sinck in martial hazards,

Too lyms, to carcasse you see what fortun is offred.
Al things goa backward : thee Gods haue flatlye renounst vs.
Oure state that whillon preserud : thee cittye to rescue,
Cleene burnt, were fruictles : let vs hardlye be slaughtred in
    armour
Tamde men haue one saulfty, not in hoap to settil a saulftye.
   Theese woords theyre valiant courradge dooe scarrifye
    deeply,
Lyke rauening woolfdams vpsoackt and gaunted in hunger,
That range in clowd shade : theyre whelps neere starued
    ar eager
And expect vdders with dry iaws : so doe we iustle :
Wee keepe thee midpath with darcknesse nightye beueyled
   Lord, bye whose heunly vttraunce may that nights blood
    be recounted ?
Or match thee misery with counteruaylabil howling ?
The old towne fals to ruin, that summers sundrye was em-
    presse.
Thee streets and kennels are with slayne carcases heaped :
Euery house, eech temple with ruful slaughter aboundeth.
And yeet thee Troians are not men vanquished onlye :
Sparcks of an old courradge to the conquourd freshlye be
    turning.
Thee Greekish victours not in eeche stroke shotfre remayned.
Loud was thee yelling, great fears and murther of al sydes.
Of Greeks thee first man with a gallant coompanye garded
Fronted vs, Androgeos, for freends vs simplye beleeuing.
In gentil manner thus he soone discoursed, vnasked.
   Hast forward feloes : what means this luskish aproching ?
You drawlach loytrers are scant from nauye repayring,
When your companions with spoyls of cittye be loaden.
   He sayd : eke on suddeyn (for he was not freendlye lik
    aunswerd)
He spyed his person with Troian coompanye wheeled,
Thence dyd he shrinck backward, his woords al softlye re-
    pressing.

Lyke when as a trauayler thee snake with brambel ycoouerd
Vnwytting squiseth, with chaunce so sudden amazed,
Speedelye whips backward from woorme, with poysoned anger
Vpsweld.   Androgeos lykwise most gastlye reculed.
Wee charge thee minions with round and compased armoure.
In streets vnknowne they doe fal, with terror apaled.
Our first encounter by fortun lucklye was ayded.
    This successe cheering and fleashing lustye Choroebus,
Thus spake he : Deere sociats, syth we haue this prosperus
        onset,
Now let vs on forward, as luck and destenye gydeth.
And let vs our targets exchange, and Greecian armour
Al clap on oure bodyes, marching with Greecian ensigne.
Craft or doughtye manhod what nice wight in foa requyreth ?
Thee Greeks shal furnish weapons. This spoken, an helmet
Of knight Androgeos glistring on pallet he pitcheth.
Hee tooke eke his target, then in hand his fawchon he griped.
Thee lyke dyd Ripheus, Dymas, and thee youthful asembly.
With new raght weapons eeche wight is newlye refreshed.
Too Greeks wee linckt vs, by Gods direction holpen.
In night shade darcknesse with foes wee skyrmished eftsoons,
And with hoat assalting too Limbo we plunged a number.
Soom run to vessels too strondward swiftlye retyring
Soom clymb theyre steeds womb, freight with perplexitye
        dastard,
Oh, Labor is fruictlesse, which Gods and destenye frustrat.
    Lo ye ; the wood virgin, with locks vnbroyded is haled
Cassandra, and trayled from temple of holye Minerua.
In vayn her eyes flamed too seat celestial heauing :
Her wrists eke tender with cord weare mannacled hardlye.
This sight foule freighted with woodful phrensye Choroebus.
Hee runs too rescu, lyk a bedlem desperat, headlong.
    Wee the man hoat foloed, wee coapt with Greekish
        asemblye.
Now be we peale pelted from tops of barbican hautye
Maynelye with our owne men by stoans downe rouled among vs.

This dolye chaunce gald vs, with blood, with slaghter
  abounding,
For that thee townsmen knew not this chaffar of armoure.
Thee Greeks al furious, too see Cassandra recoouerd,
Dyd band too geather : but chief thee courraged Aiax
And both the Atridans, thee stout Deloponian armye.
Lyke wrastling meete winds with blast contrarius huzing,
East, weast and Southwynd, with pufroare mightelye ramping,
Hudge trees downe trample: theare with God Neptun awaked
Thee seas with chauffing and strecht mace merciles hoyseth.
  Also such old enymyes: policy that former aflighted
And coucht in corners, with a vengaunce freshly retyred,
And first discoouerd thee shields and treacherye feigned.
Our speech eke and gybbrish theyre guesh dyd fortefye
  soothlye.
Down cooms thee countrey: wheare first thee sturdye
  Chorœbus
By syr Peneleus was slayne, neere consecrat altar
Of the Godesse Pallas : Ripheus lyke villenye suffred.
A man too pietee, to iustice whoalye relying.
So Gods ordayned thee chaunce. Lo oure coompanye
  slaughtred
Both Dymas and Hypanis : nor thy deuotion holye
Could salue thee Panthus, nor crowne of blissed Apollo.
You boans of Troians and houses flamed I wytnesse,
In this last byckring I shrunck no danger or hazard,
With Greeks encountring : and yf so fats had apoincted,
My fist deserued my deeath. From thence we be tumbled
Iphitus and Pelias iump with me. But Iphitus aged
Dragd, and eke Pelias sore maymd with wound of Vlisses.
  To Priamus castel thee shout doth vs hastelye carrye :
Heere was hoat assaulting, as thogh no skyrmish had els
  wheare
Beene, ne yet a subiect Troian throgh cittye wear harmed.
Thus we se Mars furiouse, thus Greeks euery harbory
  scaling,

Vp fretting the pilers, warding long wymbeled entryes.
They clinge thee scalinges too wals, and vnder a sowgard
They clymb, in lefthand, with shields, tools fellye rebating,
With righthands grapling thee tops of turret ar holden.
In valiant coombat thee Troians sturdye resisted.
They pashe thee pallets of Greeks, and rumble a muster
Of torne razte turrets, and for defensibil armoure
Thee Greeks with rold stoans in last extremitye crusshed.
And ritch gylt rafters, thee badge, thee glorius ensigne
Of blood, thee Troians are straynd too scatter in hurling.
Soom bands of Troians with weapons naked in entryes
Ranck close too geather, thee Greeks most manlye repealing.
Wee with al encoraged weare sturd too fortefye castel
Of poore king Priamus, bringing fresh streingth to the
      vanquisht.
    Theare stood an od corner from vulgar companye singled,
A posterne secret, to the castel Princelye belonging
Andromachee the woful that passage traced had often
Priuat, whilst Priamus kingdoom with saulftye remayned,
Too graundsyre leading her yoong chield Astyanacta.
Too the typ of turrets I ran, wheare feeblye the Troians
Cleene tyrde, the assaultours with weak force vaynely
      repulsed.
Theare was a toure standing on a rock, that in altitud euened
Thee stars, too seming (whence al thee Troian asemblye
Was woont thee Greek fleet to behold, and customed armye)
Wee that disioyncted; from stoans thee tymber a sunder
Wee tearde; thee ioyncturs vnknit, with an horribil hurring
Pat fals thee turret, thee Greeks with crash swash yt heapeth.
Theyre rowme supply oothers; no kind of weapon is absent,
Nor stoans, nor boans.
Theare stood ek al furiouse with wrath dan Pyrrhus in entrye
With brandisht weapons ruffling, in brasshaped armoure.
Much lyke the owtpeaking from weeds of poysoned adder,
Whom nauil of boorrows in wynters season hath harbourd.
His slougth vncasing, hym self now youthfulye bleacheth,

His tayle smoog thirling, slyke breast to Titan vpheauing.
With toonge three forcked furth spirts fyre freshlye regendred.
Theare foght Syr Periphas, and coachman of old of Achilles
Automedon named, soomtyme that guided his horses.
With theese stout captayns thee youth of Scyria marched,
They doe pres on forward, vp fire to the rafter is hurled.
In person Pyrrhus with fast wroght twibbil in handling
Downe beats with pealing thee doors, and post metal
      heaueth,
Hudge beams hee brusteth, strong bars fast ioyncted he
      renteth.
A broad gap yawning with theese great pusshes is opned,
Where with thee chambers ar playne discoouered inward.
Now Priamus parlours, with long antiquitye nobled,
Too the foa stand open, with large far gallerye stretched.
Stronglye the first entry thee Troians garded in armoure.
But the inner lodgins dyd shrille with clamorus howting,
Too skyes swift climbing was sent thee terribil owtcrye.
Then shiuering moothers throgh court doo wander agasted,
Thee posts fast colling, the pilers moste hertelye bussing.
With father his courradge his might dan Pyrrhus enhaunceth,
No man, no morter can his onset forcibil hynder.
With rip rap bouncing thee ram to the chapter is hurled,
Postes al and parlours vp from foundation heauing.
Pyks make thee passadge : and top syd turuye be turned
Al thee Princelye thrasholds ; thee Troians roundlye be
      murthred.
No place or od corners of Greekish souldor ar emptye.
Not so great a ruffling the riuer strong flasshye reteyneth
Through the breach owt spurging, eke against bancks sturdely
      shogging
It brayeth in snorting, throgh towns through countrye re-
      mouing
Both stabil and oxen.   There I saw in boucherye bathed
Fyrye Neoptolemus, both breatherne lyncked Atridans.
And Hecuba old Princesse dyd I see, with number, an hundred

Law daughters : Priamus with blood defiled his own fyre,
That with his owne traueling too Gods hee setled on altars.
Fiftye nephew striplings, and lemmans fiftye reteynd he.
Now thee statelyc pilers with gould of Barbarye fretted
Are razde.   Wheare flaming dooth cease, thear Greeks doe
    make hauock.
    Happlye what eende Priamus dyd make, now wyl be re-
    quyred.
His foes old Priamus throgh court and cittye beholding
On rusty shoulders sloa clapt his vnusual armoure,
And bootelesse morglay to his sydes hee belted vnhable.
His lif amydst the enymyes with foyne too finnish he myndeth.
In medil of the palaice to skyes broad al open an altar
Stood with greene laurel, throgh long antiquitye, shaded.
Now to this hold Hecuba, and her daughters mourneful
    asembled
In vayne for succoure gryping theyre mystical idols.
Lyke dooues in tempest clinging fast closlye to geather.
When shee shaw Priamus yoouthlyk surcharged in armoure
Shee sayd : What madnesse thee leads, vnfortunat husband,
With theese mayls massiue to be clogd ?   Now whither I
    pray the ?
Our state eke and persons may not thus weaklye be shielded.
No thogh my darling were present, courraged Hector.
Heere pitch thy fortresse : let trust be reposed in altar :
This shal vs al succour, or wee wyl ioynctlye be murthred.
This sayd ; her old husband in sacred seat she reposed.
    But se ye, from Pyrrhus scaping thee yoithlye Polytes,
Soon too king Priamus, through thrusting forcibil armoure
Rusht by long entreys, thee passadge blooddye begoaring.
Hym quick dan Pyrrhus pursuing greedelye reatcheth.
With the push and poaking of launce hee perceth his entrayls.
In sight of thee soarye parents hee fel to the groundward,
And liefe with the gushing bloodshed to the Gods he released.
When that king Priamus dyd see this boucherye beastlye,
Thogh that he were posting in fatal iournye to deaths doore

Yeet this quick cholerick challenge hee could not abandon.
  Now for this tyrany, thee Gods (so that equitye raigneth
And the loare of iustice) take, I pray theym, rightlye reueng-
    ment.
In father his presence with spightful villenye cancred,
Thee soon that murthrest, my sight with, boucherye stayning.
Not so the right valeant (whose soon thwart feigned) Achilles
Was to his foa Priamus, but laws of martial armes
Tendring, dyd render too tumb thee carcas of Hector.
And me to my kingdoom both gently and truely returned.
  The old man thus bawling, in streingth cleene weakned,
    here hurled
His dart at Pyrrhus from the armoure feeblye rebounding,
In bos of his target with flagging weaknes yt hangeth.
  Whye then, quod Pyrrhus, thow shalt bee speedely posted
Too coast infernal, thear let my exployts be reported.
My father aduertise, that I was ful truelye begotten,
Baselye Neoptolemus was borne, that carrye for errand.
  This sayd, poor Priamus with force from the altar is haled,
And then syr Pyrrhus with left hand grapled his hoarelocks,
In the blud hym ducking of his owne soon, sellye Polytes.
His blad he with thrusting in his old dwynd carcas vphilted.
This was Prince Priamus last ende and desteny final,
Who saw thee Troians vanquisht, thee cittye repressed :
Empror of hudge Asia, earst ruling with dignitye regal,
In shoare now namelesse dooth ly lyke a trunchon al head-
    lesse.
  This when I perceaued, with sensibil horror atached,
My father Anchises heere with do I cal to remembraunce,
Whilst I beheld Priamus thus gasping, my syre his adgemate,
I beare eke in memorye my wiefe left soalye Creüsa.
And my house dispoyled, then I thinck on my soon Iülus.
In this wise musing myn eye glaunst to my coompanye fensiue,
I doe spye no Troian, for soom tyerde, tumbled al headlong
Too ground, and diuerse were burnt with purposed offer.
Thus then I left naked, by vestaes temple abyding

False Helen, in lurcking manner close setled, I marcked.
Thee flaming brightnesse from sight dooth darcknes abandon.
This minion doubting thee Troians blooddye reuengment,
And also fearing thee Greckish fyrie requital,
Thee bane of vs Troians, of Greeks thee mak bate Erinnys,
Formd her in a corner sneaking detested of altars.
With choler inflaming I rest al restles in anger,
With the death of the lady to requit my countrye repressed.
   To Mycen, or Spartans and shal she be saulfly returned?
And after conquest as Queene with glorye to floorish?
Her father, her palaces shal shee se, her children, her hus-
   band?
With the knot of Troian matrons to her seruice alotted?
Slayn lyes king Priamus: thee Troian citye beskorched.
Thee shoars of Dardan for her oft with bloodshed abounded.
No suer, I may not such an horribil iniurye cancel.
For to kil a woonman thogh no greate glorye be gleamed,
Thogh valor and al honoure from suche weake victorye flitteth,
Yeet to slea this fryrebrand, of al hurly burlye the foundresse,
Must bee commended.   My mynd eke further is eased
Yf that of oure slaughters I shal bee partlye reuenged.
   And as I thus muttred, with roystring phrensye betraynted
My moother, the Godesse (who was accustomed algats
Eare this tyme present to be dusk) most brimlye dyd offer
Her self to visadge, thee night with brightnes auoyding.
Eeune lyk as her deitee to the Sainets dooth luster in heun-
   blisse.
Shee claspt my righthand, her sweet rose parlye thus adding.
   Soon to what od purpose thus meane ye to ruffle in anger?
What maks you furious? wyl you care charye relinquish
Of mee youre moother?   Too post with speedines hoamward
Too father Anchises were best: yf seallye Creüsa
Or the lad Ascanius from murder saulflye be breathing.
Theym Greeks assalting had kild, or turned in ashes
Had not my deitee theyre streingth ouer highlye resisted.
Not thee Greekish Helen (whose sight thy passion angrye

Enkendleth) not fautye Paris this cittye represseth.
This ruin ordeyned thee Gods and destenye froward.
Looke (for I thee moysture whearwith,now mortal, is hyndred
Thy sight, doo bannish, thee darcknesse clowdye remoouing.
See, that you doe folow youre moothers destinat order,
What she the commaundeth to obserue, preciselye remember)
Heere loa, whear heaps hudgy thow seest disioyncted a sunder
And stoans dismembred from stoans, smooke foggye bedusted,
Thee wals God Neptune, with mace threeforcked, vphurleth,
And cleene theire ioyncturs from deepe foundation heaueth.
And the Godesse Iuno ful fraight with pooysoned enuye
Thee gates strong warding, furth from the nauye the Greek
   foas
Dooth whoup, streight belted with steele.
In tops of turrets see wheare Tritonia Pallas
Is set, thee Troians killing with Gorgon his eyesight.
Thee father of deitee thee Greeks dooth mightelye courradge :
Through his procurement thee Gods thee cittye dishable.
Flee, fle, my sweet darling, let toyls bee finnished hastly.
Thow shalt bee shielded with my protection alway.
I wil not fayle thee to tyme thow saulflye be setled.
   This sayd, with darcksoom night shade quite clowdye she
      vannisht.
Grislye faces frouncing, eke agaynst Troy leaged in hatred
Of Saincts soure deitees dyd I see.
Then dyd I marck playnely thee castel of Ilion vplayd,
And Troian buyldings quit topsy turuye remooued.
Much lyk on a mountayn thee tree dry wythered oaken
Sliest by the clowne Coridon rusticks with twibbil, or hatchet.
Then the tre deepe minced, far chopt dooth terrifye swinckers,
With menacing becking thee branches palsye beforetyme,
Vntil with sowghing yt grunts, as wounded in hacking.
At leingth with rounsefal, from stock vntruncked, yt harssheth.
   With Gods assistaunce downe from thee turret I lighted,
Mye tools make passadge through flame and hostilitye
   Greekish.

Too father Anchises old house thus saulflye retyred,
Foorth with I dyd purpose from thence too desolat hiltops
My syre too carry, but as I this matter had vttred,
Too liue now longer, Troy burnt, hee flatlye reneaged ;
Or to dwel as bannisht. But, he sayd, you lustye iuuentus
In yeers and carcasse prime, quick and liuelye remayning
Flee you.
If Gods omnipotent my lief too linger had ordred
They would theese lodgings haue fenst. Sufficeth yt also
That Troians misery dyd I liue too testifye mourneful.
Good syrs, bee packing, let my corps heere be reposed.
My fist shal purchase my death, my foa mercye wyl offer
For thee bootye fishing. Of graue to be voyded is harmelesse.
Long my liefe I pampred, too Gods celestial yrksoom,
Syth king of mankind, father of diuinitye total,
With thundring lightnings, my carcasse stronglye beblasted.
    Theese woords expressing in one heast hee stieflye remayned
Round fel I too weeping, with my spouse soarye Creüsa,
With my soon Ascanius, with al eke thee sorroful houshold.
Hym we al desyred too tame this desperat owtrage,
Oure final slaghter not with such follye to purchase.
Hee rested wylful lyk a wayward obstinat oldgrey.
I then alarm shouted, too dy dyd I verelye purpose,
For now what counsayl, what course may rightlye be taken ?
    What ? father Anchises, hold you my duitye so sclender,
Too slip from Troytowne, and heere you soole to relinquish ?
From the fathers sermons shal such fond patcherye flicker ?
If Gods eternal thee last disseuered offal
Of Troy determyn too burne, yf you father also
Youre self too murther, too roote youre progenye purpose,
Catch that catch may be, thee street gate to slaghter is open.
From killing Priamus, dan Pyrrhus shortlye wyl hither,
Thee soon fast bye the syre ; thee syre that murthred at
    altars.
Wasd for this (moother) that mee throgh danger vnharmed
You led, now my enymyes to behold too riffle in hous seat ?

And my soon Ascanius, my syre, my seallye Creusa
For to se deepe bathed, grooueling in bloods of eche oother?
Nay then I beeshrew me : make ye hast syrs : bring me myn
  armoure.
Now for a last farewel do I take me to Greekish asembly.
Soom Greeks shal find yt bitter, before al we be slaghtred.
I girt my weapons to my syde, my tergat I setled
On lift hand so rushing to the streets I posted in anger.
But my feete embracing my pheere me in the entrye reteyned.
Too father owtraging thee soon shee tendred Iulus.

  If to dye you purpose, take vs also in coompanye with you.
If through experience soom trust ye doe settel in armoure
First gard this dwelling, wheare rests thee childish Iulus,
Wheare father is seated, where youre spouse named, is har-
  bourd.
  Theese woords owt showting, with her howling the house
    she replennisht
But look, on a suddeyn what chaunce most woonderus hapned
Tweene father and moother thee yong boy setled Iulus,
A certeyn lightning on his headtop glistered harmclesse.
His crisp locks frizeling, his temples prittelye stroaking.
Heer with al in trembling with speede wee ruffled his hearebush,
With water attempting thee flame too mortifye sacred.
But father Anchises, mounting his sight to the skyward,
Both the hands vplifting, hertly thus his orison vttred.

  Iuppiter omnipotent (yf that prayer annye the bendeth)
Vs pitye, thy seruaunts, yf eke oght our godlines asketh,
Graunt (father) assiistaunce this mirracle happye to stablish.
  Scant had he this finnisht, when that, with sudden, a
    thundring
In the skye dyd rumble, foorth with theire flamed a blazing
Star, streams owt shooting, yeelding of cleerenes abundaunce.
Wee noted yt glyding from tops of mansion houseplace.
Lastlye the star sincking in woods wyde of Ida was hydden,
Right the waye furth poincting. Thee wood with brightnes
  apeereth.

Eech path was fulsoom with sent of sulphurus orpyn.
My father heere conquerd, hymself vp lustelye lifted.
With the Godhead parling, he the star crinital adoreth.
 Now, quod he, no lingring, let vs hence, I am prest to be
  packing.
Saulfe my prittye nephew, you Gods of countrye, my linnadge.
You do manadge Troytowne, this is eke your prosperus omen.
Now, my soon, on forward, thy syre is prest hastlye to track
  thee.
 Thus sayd he.   Thee flaming to the townewals more nerc
  aproched,
And the flash of burning with skorching speedines hasted.
Wel father in Gods name, mount on my shoulder, I pray you.
This labor is pleasaunt, to me t'ys not payneful or yrcksoom.
What luck shal betyde vs, wee wyl be in destenye partners,
Or good hap, or froward : and let my young lad Iulus
Next be my companion, my wief may softlye pace after.
Syrs, you thee seruaunts, slack not my woords to remember.
A tumb to Troytowne and mouldy tempil aneereth
Vowd to the godly Ceres, a ciper by the churche seat abydeth
By oure old progeniotours long tyme deuoutlye regarded.
From diuersc corners to that hewt wee wyl make asemblye.
Gripe, father, oure country deitees, se ye warelye keepe theym.
For sith I with byckrings embrewd so blooddye my fingers,
I may not, I dare not pollute Gods heaunlye, with handling,
Vntil I with fountayn mee wash.
 When that I theese speeches deliuered, I twisted a wallet
On my broad shoulders, my nape dyd I settle eke vnder,
With lion his yellow darck skyn my carcase I cased.
My father on shouldeers I set, my yoong lad Iülus
I lead with righthand, tripping with pit pat vnequal,
My wiefe cooms after, through crosse blynd allye we iumble.
And I that in forenight was with no weapon agasted,
And litel esteemed thee swarms of Greekish asemblye
Now shiuer at shaddows, eeche pipling puf doth amaze me.
For yong companion, for bedred burden abashed.

Danger al escaping to the gats I saulflye repayred.
Yeet not with standing a trampling sudden of hoatfoot
Soldours vs chased, to my thincking ; my father also
Casting eye backward cryed owt, soon fle, they doe track vs.
I doe se theyre brandisht tergats, and brasshapen harneise.
Now was I from policy fore cast with terror amooued,
For whilst I wandred through streets and passages vncooth,
My wief departed, my coomfort hertye Creüsa.
Yf death her had goared, she behynd yf weerye remayned,
Or strayed in foloing, I knew not truelye : but after
Vnseene she rested, nor backward skewd I myn ejesight,
In graue of holy Ceres tyl that my burden I lighted.
For shee was missing, when al our good coompanye clustred.
With soon, with famely, with mee shee kept not apoinctment.
Too Gods, too creaturs I belcht owt blasphemye bawling.
For to me what mischief could chaunce in cittye more hurtful.
My father Anchises, my chield I took to my seruaunts,
And Gods of Troians were coucht in custodye secret.
I to the towne turned close clad with burnished armoure,
I was determind fully, too ventur al hazards,
Al Troy too trauerse, too suffer danger al hapning.
First dyd I coom backward to the wals, from whence I
    remooued,
Too the gat I posted by night, and carefulye dogging
Thee way with lightflams, eeche crooked corner I ransackt.
Both with night ye silence was I quayled and greatlye with
    horror.
Thence dyd I trudge hoamward, too learne yf she haplye
    returned.
But theare weare the enymyes with thronging cluster
    asembled.
Thee fyre heer on fretting with blaze too rafter is heaued.
Thee flams surmounting tenements doo whize to the skyward.
I ran too Priamus razd court, at castel I gazed,
In cels and temple, that of old too Iuno was apted.
As keeper Phœnix was made, with ruthles Vlisses

Of booty and pillage. Theere Troian treasur is hurded,
That flames escaped, thear stood the rich halloed altars.
Theare massiue gould cups bee layd, theare wardrob abundant
Of roabs most pretiouse, thear ar eke yoong children in order
With cold hert moothers, for Greekish victorye quaking,
Setled on al sydes.
I stoutly emboldned with night shade raysed an howting,
With mournful belling I namde expreslye, Creüsa.
In vayne with sobbing was oft that od eccho repeated.
In this guise frantyck as I ran throgh cittye with howling
I noted on suddeyn the goast of verye Creüsa,
And her woonted image, to me knowne, mad her elfish
    aparance.
Heere with I was daunted, my hear stard, and speechles I
    stutted.
Then to me thus speaking, my carck in search she remooued.
    This labor, ô husband, too no great purpose auayleth,
For this hap is chaunced bye the Gods prefixed apoinctment.
Hence yt is vnlawful with you too carrye Creüsa.
That trauayl is shortned by the king of sacred Olympus.
Thow must with surges bee banged and pilgrimage yrcksoom.
In land Hesperian thow shalt bee saulflye receaued,
Wheare glydes throgh cornefilds, with streaming secrecye,
    Tybris.
Theare doe lye great kingdooms, and Queene most Princelye
    bespoken
For the, mye kind husband for mee grief therefor abandon.
Now me the Myrmidones for captiue prisoner hold not,
Nor sterne snuff Dolopans, and Greekish matron I serue not,
Of Venus in wedlock thee daughter.
Of Gods thee moother me in this my countrye reteyneth.
Fare ye wel, ô husband, oure yoong babye charely tender.
    This sayd, shee vannisht, and thogh that I sadlye requyred,
Too confer further, yeet shee too tarrye renounced.
Thryce dyd I theare coouet, to col, to clasp her in armes.
Thryce then thee spirit my catching swiftlye refused.

Much lyk to a pufwynd, or nap that vannished hastlye.
Thee twylight twinckled, furth I to my coompanye posted.
Whear soone I perceiued with woonder a multitud hudgye.
Of men with woomen too this layre newlye repayred.
Thee yoonger Troians, thee meaner wretched asemblye
Round to me dyd cluster, with purse and person abyding
Prest, throgh surgye waters with mee too seek ther auenturs.
Lucifer owtpeaking in tips of mounted hil Ida
On draws thee dawning. Thee Greeks with custodye watchful,
Warded thee towngats, hoap here of no succor abydeth.
I shrunck, and my father to the crowne of mounten I lifted.

Finis libri secundi.

THEE THIRD
BOOKE OF VIR-
GIL HIS ÆNEIS.

Hen giltlesse Asian kingdoom sterne destenye quasshed,
With Priamus country when squysd was the Ilian empyre,
When Troy was razed, quight from foundation hoysed :
Furth to run exiled, too seeke soom forren auentures,
By Gods we are warned. Wee rigd our nauye flat vnder
Haut hil of Antander, not far from mounten of Ida.
Then we wer vncerteyn too what saulf soyle to betake vs.
Men to vs thick crouded : scant was prime summer aproched,
When father Anchises to the seas thee coompanye charged.
I, salt tears shedding, my natiue countrye relinquisht,
Thee roads and platfourms where Troy stood : sad to the seaward
With my companions and with my yoong son Iülus
With Gods, mightye patrons, my course and passage I bended.
A large wyld region theare stands, Mauortia cleaped,
Thracia sum terme yt : theare raignd thee bluddye Lycurgus :
Thee Troian leage seat, with fastned freendship abyding
Whilst fortune floated. With crosse blast thither I sayled,
On shore eke I founded townewals, by destenye lucklesse :

Of my name, Æneidans dwellers, theare setled, I named.
Too Venus and the sacred remnaunt of thee holye trium-
     phaunts
I framd a sacrifice, the begun wurck lucklye toe prosper,
And toe Ioue omnipotent a bul neere seaside I slaughtred.
A tumb theare rested by chaunce close shaded al vpward
With twigs thick crumpled, with myrtel mossye thear edging.
I drew neere, mynding too roote fro cel earthye the thicket,
With thee slips greenish too deck thee new shaped altars.
I viewd with wundring a grisly monsterus hazard.
For the tre supplanted, that first fro the roote seat is haled,
With drop drop trilling of swart blud filtred abundance.
Thee ground black steyning: then furth with a quiuerish
     horror
My ioyncts child ransackt, my blud with terror apaling.
At the secund pulling, when an oother wicker is vp pluckt.
Thearbye the whole matter furth with more deepelye to ferret,
From that stub lykewise foorth spirt drops bluddelye stilling.
With this hap entangled, thee sweete Nymphs rural I woor-
     shipt,
And God Mars the Regent of that soyle crabbed adoring,
Too turne too goodnesse this sight and merciles omen.
But when I thee third tyme with grype more fiercelye dyd
     offer,
Ny knees fast pitching on sands, too pluck vp an oother:
(What? shal I chat further? from speeche shal secrecye bar
     mee?)
From pits deepe bottoom dooth skritche a woonderus howling,
With playnts most pitiful to oure ears thus sadlye rebounding.
Woorthye syr Æneas, why with this boutcherye teare you
A caytiefe forlorne?   Extend your mercye to deadfolck.
Foule not your sacred hands: you rack no forrener owtcast,
You rent a Troian: theese drops from shrubs doe not issue.
Oh, flee this Canibal country, this coouetus Island.
I am named syr Polydor; with darts fel nayled heer vnder
I lodge: which thicket thus growne me terriblye stingeth.

I stud al astonyed, my hear starde, and speechles I rested.
This Polydor whillon with pure gould mightelye loaden,
Preeuelye by Priamus, thee Troian rector vnhappye,
Too king Treicius was sent, to be charelye noozeld.
But when this gardein perceu'd the aduersitye Troian,
And that theyre citty thee Grecian armye besieged ;
Heee leaues thee conquourd, and clingd to the partye trium-
     phant.
Al trust fowlye breaking, thee poore Polydorus is headlesse
Through wycked murther, thee gould thee traytor vp hurdeth.
What feat or endeuours of gould thow consecrat hungar
Mens mynds constrainst not with wyels or vertue to coom-
     passe.
When that I tooke courradge, when pangs al feareful I ban-
     nisht,
I told thee chiefteyns, and namelye my good father adged
This strange aduenture, theyre iudgements also requyring.
Swiftlye they determind too flee from a countrye so wycked,
Paltocks Inne leauing, too wrinche thee nauye too southward.
For polydor wee framd an obit : wee tumbled in heapwise
Of stoans a cluster, with black weede the altar is hanged,
With tree swartye Cipers : Troy dames with customed vsadge
Trol round, downe tracing with theyre discheaueled hearlocks.
Wee poured mylck luke warme foaming, and blud sacred after.
With mayne noise lifted to the slayne soule lastlye we shouted.
When soft gale sootherne and calme seas saulftye dyd offer,
My mates lancht forward theyre fleete, from shoare we be
     glyding,
Thee roads, thee countrey, thee towns fro oure nauye be
     gadding.
  In the myd of the searowme theare stands a plentiful Island
Too thee dame of myrmayds, too Neptune Princelye relying.
This was roundlye bayed (for so the Ioue heunlye dyd order)
With Mycone, and eke with Giarus, two famosed Islands.
Theare resting habitants no wynd flaws stormye regarded.
Too this Ile I sayled, wee saulflye dyd harbor in hauen.

When we were al landed, we the cittye of Phœbus adored.
King Anius, king of the habitants, and priest of Apollo.
Crownd with fresh garland, with laurels consecrat headband,
Glad met vs, also knowing Anchises adged, his old freend.
Theare we shake hands kyndly, foorth with we are setled in
    hostrye.
In the old buylt tempil thus thee God Phœbus I woorshipt.
    Soom bye place of resting graunt vs, most sacred Apollo,
Yeeld wals too vs wery, soom stock, soom towne for abyding,
Saulue the secund Troytowne, thee scraaps of wrathful
    Achilles,
Of Greeks thee rellicks ; by what king shal we be ruled ?
What man is our captayne ? Too what soyle worldlye to
    iourney,
Thow doost commaund vs ? where shal we be lastlye reposed ?
Shew father a prophecy ; poure downe thye good oracle heunly.
    Scant had I thus spoken, when seats al quiuered about vs.
Thee doors, thee laurel, thee mount with terribil earth quake
Doo totter shiuering, with rumbling mutterus eccho.
Then to vs squat grooueling in this wise the oracle aunswerd.
    You brawnd hard Troians, what soyle youre auncetrye seised
First of al old countreys, to the same you shal be reduced.
Track owt youre moother, whom long antiquytye graunted.
With seed of Æneas shal coompasse earthlye be ruled.
His soons soons and soons from their braue progenye
    springing.
    Thus God Apollo cryed : but wee with an vnison outcrye,
And with iollye tumult, where should that cittye be setled
Streight ways demaunded, what place God Phœbus apoincted,
    My father Achises vp al old antiquitye ripping,
Heare me, quod hee, lordinges, lerne the expectation hoaped.
Thee Creet Ile in mydseas dooth stand too Iuppiter hallowd :
Theare mount Ide resteth, thee springe of progenye Troian.
A fruictful kingdoam, with towns in number an hundred.
Hence our progenitour (so I fayle not in historye told mee)
Surnamed Teucrus first came too Rhetean Island.

Theare picht he his kingdoom, for then Troy cittye was
    vnbuylt,
And castels stood not, the habitans in vallye remayned.
Theare dwelt dame Cybele in forrest of desolat Ida.
And moonewise Coribants on brasse their od harmonye
    tinckling.
Thence cooms trustye silence vsd in sollemnitye sacred.
And two stately lyons this fine dams gilt wagon haled.
Wisely let vs thearefor too Gods direction harcken:
Let wynds be swadged foorth with, too Candye be packing.
Short is thee passadge (so that oure God Iuppiter help vs)
In three days sayling wee shal too Candye be puffed.
    This discourse eended, too the altars holye returning,
A Bul too Neptune, wyth a bul too golden Apollo,
Hee lykewise slaughtred too roaring wynter a blackbeast,
But to the sweet west wynd a best whit lillye was offred.
    Theare fleeth a rumoure, that king of Candye relinquisht
His seat, that the Island is left vnfurnished holye.
Wee left Ortigian countrey, with nauye we passed
By mounts of Nazon too skincking Bacchus alotted.
From thence wee trauayled to the greenedeckt gaylye Donysa:
To Olcoron, too lillye Paron, to the Cyclades also
Dispersd and scatterd, and neere creeks sundrye we sayled.
    Thee thickskyn mariners shouted with sudden agreement.
My maats assented to bend too Candye the passadge.
Thee wynd puft forward with sweete gale freelye the nauye:
At leingth by sayling on land of Candye we lighted.
First then at oure landing towne wals I ther hastelye founded.
Pergamea I cald yt, that name they gladlye receaued.
By me they were counsayld too buyld vp sumptuus houses.
Also bye this season too docks oure nauye was haled.
Thee youth too wedlock and tylladge thriftelye clustred.
Both laws and tenements I framd. But streight on a suddein
A plagye boch ranged, with foule contagion ayrye
Both bodyes festring and fruict trees plentiful harming.
A yeere too dismal. For sweete lief swiftlye was eended,

Thee fields cleene fruictlesse thee dogstar Sirius heated.
Thee flours wax withred, thee soyle fruicts plentye renegeth.
My father exhorted too turne too sacred Apollo,
For toe craue our pardon, when should this iournye be finnisht,
Or trauail expyred, by what means might we be furthred.
  Thee night his mantel dooth spred: with slumber is holden
Eche liuing creature, then my holye domestical housgods,
In last nights fyrebroyls, that from Troy skorched I saulued,
In glistred shyning in a dreame toe me made thear aparaunce.
Inmp at thee wyndoors, where moonshyne brimlye dyd enter.
Thus to me they parled, shredding of sorroful anguish.
  Syr, to ye what soothsay to record dooth purpose Apollo,
Heere that he dischargeth: we be sent too signify his errand
Wee skapte from Troybrands bye thye courradge manfulye
    shielded
And bye thye good guiding through seaplash stormye we
    marched.
Wee thee same pilgrims wyl yeeld to thye progenye glorye,
And rule too citty.   Let townewals mightye be raised
Streight by the for mighty persons: let no reason hold thee
From flight: this countrey must be forsaken: Apollo
Ment not, in his prophecy, thy course too Candye to further.
Theare stands a region, by Greeks yt is Hesperye named,
A stout old countrey, with plenty fertil abounding.
Theare dwelt th'Ænotrians, but now by the coompanye yonger
Of thee first captayn valiaunt, yt is Italye termed:
Oure seat thear resteth: theare borne was Dardanus adged,
And father Iäsius: from whence oure auncetrye sprouted.
Wherefor in al gladnesse to thyne old sire certifye tydings:
Skud to soyl Italian, from Candye the Iuppiter haleth.
  With theese Gods gingling, with sight moste geason apaled,
(For to mye ful seeming with slumber I was not atached
I knew theire tucktlocks, I knew their phisnomye present
A cold sweat saltish through my ioynctes fiercely dyd enter)
From my bed I started: to the sky with meeknes I lifted
My hands deuoutlye praying, then too my fortunat housgods

I framd a sacrifice : next with ioy tickled I posted
Too my syre Anchises : and told thee matter in order.
Hee noted his stumbling to haue coom from the auncetrye
    doubtful.
And dubil acceptaunce of syers to haue fostred his erroure.
    O my son Æneas, with Troian destenye toughned ;
Thee self same prophecy too mee Cassandra recited:
Now cal I too memory that shee this countrye remembred,
Often at Hesperian regions, and Italye glauncing.
But to soyl Hesperian that Troymen should be remooued,
What wight coniecturde ? who would Cassandra then harcken?
Accept wee therefor this course, and credit Apollo.
    Thus sayd : we assented to his lore with cheereful
        obeysaunce.
Wee leaue Creete country ; and our sayls vnwrapped vphoysing,
With woodden vessel thee rough seas deepelye we furrowe.
When we fro land harbours too mayne seas gyddye dyd enter
Voyded of al coast sight with wild fluds roundly bebayed,
A watrye clowd gloomming, ful aboue mee clampred, apeered,
A sharp storme menacing, from sight beams soonnye reiecting:
Thee flaws with rumbling, thee wroght fluds angrye doe
        iumble :
Vp swel thee surges, in chauffe sea plasshye we tumble :
With the rayn, is daylight through darcknesse mostye
        bewrapped,
And thundring lightbolts from torneclowds fyrye be flasshing.
Wee doe mis oure passadge through fel fluds boysterus erring,
Oure pilot eke, Palinure, through dymnesse clowdye bedusked
In poinccts of coompasse dooth stray with palpabil erroure.
Three dayes in darcknesse from bright beams soony repealed,
And three nigths parted from lightning starrye we wandred.
Thee fourth day foloing thee shoare, neere setled, apeered
And hils vppeaking ; and smoak swift steamd to the skyward.
Oure sayls are strucken, we roa furth with speedines hastye,
And the sea by our mariners with the oars cleene canted is
        harrowd

On shoars of strophades from storme escaped I landed,
For those plats Strophades in languadge Greekish ar highted,
With the sea coucht Islands. Where foule bird foggye Celæno
And Harpy is nestled : sence franckling Phines his housroume
From theym was sunderd, and fragments plentye remooued.
No plage more perilous, no monster grislye more ouglye,
No stigian vengaunce lyke too theese carmoran haggards.
Theese fouls lyke maydens are pynde with phisnomye palish ;
With ramd cramd garbadge, theire gorges draftye be gulled,
With tallants prowling, theire face wan withred in hunger,
With famin vpsoaken.
When tward theese Islands oure ships wee setled in hauen,
Neere, we viewd, grasing heards of bigge franckye fat oxen,
And goats eke cropping carelesse, not garded of heerdman.
Wee rusht with weapons, parte of thee bootye we lotted
First to Ioue. On banck syds our selues with food we reposed.
But loa with a suddeyn flushing thee gulligut harpeys
From mountayns flitter, with gagling whirlerye flapping
Theyr wings : furth the viand fro tabils al greedelye snatching,
With fulsoom sauour, with stincking poysoned ordure
Thee ground they smeared, theartoo skriches harshye re-
    ioyning.
Then we set al the tabils, and fyrde oure mystical altars
Vnder a rock arched, with trees thick coouered ouer.
At the secund sitting from parcels sundrye repayred
This cooui rauenouse, and swift with a desperat onset,
They gripte in tallants the meat and furth spourged a
    stincking
Foule carrayne sauoure: then I wild thee coompanye present,
Too take theire weapons, and fight with mischeuus howlets.
My wyl at a beckning is doon, they doe run to ther armoure
In grasse theyre flachets, and tergats warelye pitching.
But when at a thurd flight theese fowls to the coompanye
    neered,
With shril brasse trumpet Misenus sowned alarum.
Oure men marcht forward, and fierce gaue a martial vncoth

Charge, theese strange vulturs with skirmish bluddye to
   mayster.
But strokes theire feathers pearsd not, nor carcases harmed:
And toe skye they soared, thee victals clammye behynd theym,
They do leaue haulf mangled with sent vnsauerye bepoudred.
On the typ of rockish turret stood gastlye Celæno
Vnlucky prophetesse; and thus she recounted her errand.
   And now Syr Troians, wyl you for slaughter of oxen
And for al our owne good wage war with sellye poore harpeys?
And vs from kingdoom banish?   Then take me this errand:
And what I shal prophecy with tentiue listenes harcken,
What Ioue too Phœbus, too me also what vttred Apollo.
I the chiefe hel fyrebrand of fel furye mischeuus holden
Wyl now discoouer thee self same mysterye told mee.
Italye you long for, to the land eke of Italye saulflye
You shal bee guided with winds, and setled in hauen.
Yeet not with standing ere conquerd cittye be rampyrde,
For this youre trespas you shal be so gaunted in hunger,
That youre smeary tabils you wyl most greedelye swallow.
   Thus she sayd: and forward to the wood shee flickered
   hastlye.
At this hap oure feloes with feareful phantasye daunted,
Stood stil al astonied with cold blud, lyke gelu, quiuering.
They doe quayl in courradge, and with no martial armoure,
But by ther holye prayers they doe practise peaceful atoane-
   ment.
If godesesse, yf byrds stincking, or bugs they resembled.
   But father Anchises his palms from strond plat inhauncing
On Gods heunlye cryeth, to ther hest with duitye relying:
Gods, quod he, this messadge turne you to a prosperus omen.
Cancel theese menacing soothings, thee godlye reseruing.
   Thus sayd: swift we weyed the anchors, and sayles vp-
   hoysed,
With northen bluster through fome seas speedelye flitting,
As the gale and the pilot with steering skylful vs haleth.
In midil of the sea deepe wee saw thee woddye Zacynthos,

Dulichium, Samee, with cragged Neritos hard stond.
Wee fle the rocks of Ithack, and coast of Princelye Laërtes,
Also we the byrth place detest of flinted Vlisses.
Thee mount Leucates with thick clowds gloommye bedawbed
Vp peaks to the viewing, with feareful poinct of Apollo.
Theare we were enshoared quight tyrde, and on to the
    borough
As we gad, oure vessels vpdrawne are grapled at anchor.
Theare we being landed saulfly through fortun vnhoaped,
Too Ioue wee sacrifice, sundry hostes are flamed on altars,
And Troian pastymes wee practise in Actean Island.
Soom feloes naked with larding smearye bebasted,
With wrastling gambalds for price, for maystrye doe struggle
Myrrye for escaping thee towns and Grecian hamlets,
Through theire deadly foes theire passage luckye recounting:
    Thee whilst fayre Phœbus thee yeers course roundlye
    reuolued,
And seas, with north blast and wynter frostye, be roughned :
A brasen hudge terget, that Abans erst fenced in armoure,
On post I nayled, thee clingde shield this posye beareth.
This Signe AEneas From Grekish Conqueror Haled.
I gaue commaundment fro the port to the ships to be packing.
My maats skum the sea froth there in oars strong cherelye
    dipping.
Thee Pheacan turrets foorth with from sight we relinquish.
Wee coast Epëirus, thence wee touche Chaön his hauen.
And to the great burrough of Butthrot statelye we skudded.
Heere, loa, throgh oure hyring a report incredibil, vncoth,
Glides, that Prince Helenus, by Troian lineal ofspring
Soon too king Priamus, this Greekish countrye reteyneth.
Thee pheere possessing and crowne of Pyrrhus his empyre,
Also that Andromachee dooth bed with a countrye man
    husband.
Theese news mee mazing, my mynd was greedelye whetned,
Too parle with the Regent, too lerne this meruelus hapning.
I stept from the hauen, leauing my nauye behynd mee.

Happelye that season soom banckets costlye, with oother
Lamenting presents (in shade to the cittye reioyning
Neere water of Simois both deepely and warelye sliding)
Andromachee framed to the dust, on tumb eke of Hector
Calling with burial yelling, that al emptye remayned :
With greene turf circled ; from thence right on she repayred,
For cause of further mourning, too consecrat altars.
When she dyd espy mee posting, and Troiecal armoure
Too too gyddye viewd, with vnordinat extasis hamperd,
Downe she fel on suddeyn, thee cold too carcas aprocheth :
Shee sowns, and after long pausing thus she sayd elflyke.

   Is thye true playne visadge with tru shape natural offred ?
Imp of a statelye Godesse bringst thou to me verelye tydings?
Art thow yeet liuing ? or the yf light worldlye relinquisht,
Tel me where is my husband, my sweeting delicat Hector ?

   Thus sayd : al in blubbring shee floath, with clamorus
         howling
Thee place shee tinckled : but I through pangs vncoth
   vnhabled,
With stutting stamering at leingth thus fumbled an aunswer.

   I doe liue, I assure thee, thogh dangers sundrye me taynted,
Doubt ye not, a changling ye se none.
Lord what good fortune thee lack of pristinat husband
Hath toe thye contentment with new match luckye releeued?
Possesseth Pyrrhus thee spouse of famosed Hector ?

   Downe she smote her visadge, to me thus ful smoothlye
         replying.
ò Priamus daughter, thee virgin Princelye, thrise happye
Thow that by thye foes neere Troy wals slaughtered hast
      beene.
By this hap escaping thee filth of lottarye carnal.
Too couche not mounting of mayster vanquisher hoatspur.
But we, by crosse passadge from flamed countrye remoued,
Thee pryde of a stripling and ymp of wrathful Achilles
Haue borne with thraldoom, with sharp captiuitye fetterd,
Hee to fyne Hermionee, for Greeks a bootye to peerelesse,

Daughter too Queene Helen, fast and hoat phantasye bended.
Me his nyefe to his seruaunt Helenus ful firmelye betroathed.
But yeet vnexpected with ialosye kendled Orestes
For los of his beadmate, dyd take too tardye my master,
Hym by his syers altars killing with skarboro warning.
When fro Neoptolemus thee vital spirit abated
This part was to Helenus by wylled parcerye lotted :
Chaönian countreys of Troian Chaön ycleaped :
This towne Troy citty, this castel eke Ilion highting.
But to the what passadge thee winds and fortun alotted ?
Or what great deity tost thee to our desolat angel ?
How faers Ascanius ? doth he liue, and breathful abydeth ?
Whom to the now Troytowne.
Dooth the los of moother to her chielde bring sorreful anguish?
Are sparcks of courradge in this yong progeny kendled
By father Æneas, with his vncle martial Hector ?
    Theese toyes she pratled mourning, griefs newlye refreshing
Thee whilst king Helenus, with a crowding coompanye garded,
From towne to vs buskling vs as his freends freendlye
    bewelcomd.
Vs to his new citty with curtesye cheereful he leadeth ;
With tears rief trickling saucing eeche question asked,
I march on forward : and yoong Troy finelye resembling
Thee big huge old monument, and new brooke Zanthus I
    knowledge.
With the petit townegats fauoring thee principal old portes.
Also mye companions in country cittye be frollickt :
In toe the verye palaice thee Prince theym wholye receaueth.
With whip cat bowling they kept a myrry carousing,
Thee goulden mazurs vp skynckt for a bon viage hoysing.
There we dyd al soiourne two dayes : then a prosperus
    hizling
Of south blast, puffing on sayles dooth summon vs onward.
Too thee Princely prophet thus I spake, hym freendlye
    requesting.
    O sacred Troian, thee light of misterye darckned,

Of Gods thee spooks make, thee truchman of hallod Apollo :
By the God enstructed by stars for to ominat eeche thing,
By flight and chirping byrds too prognosticat aptlye :
Poure foorth thy prophecy (for too mee prosperus hazards
Eeche sound relligion foretold, mee to Italye posting,
Only on displeasaunt foule shapte byrd, the Harpye Celæno
(Forwarns much mischiefe too coom with dangerus hunger)
In theese stormye perils too what saulf porte shal I take mee ?
     King Helenus slaughtring, with woont accustomed heyfers,
Peace craues of the Godhead, from front thee label vnhanging,
Mee, by the hand, trembling hee leads to thye mysterye
     (Phœbus)
Thee priest this prophecy from Gods direction opned.
     Thow soon of holye Venus (for th'art by setled apoinct-
     ment
Of Gods mightye power to exploits most doughtye reserued,
Thus thy fate establisht dooth rest, so thye fortun is ordred)
Of poincts sundrye wyl I to the shape but a curtal abridg-
     ment,
Too the eende in thye trauayl thow mayst the more heedlye
     be lessond,
And passe to Italian region, thus shortlye rehersing
Peece meale prittye parings : for, too tel a summarye total.
Thee fat's king Helenus dooe bar, with Iuno the Saturne.
Wheare thow supposest therefor, that here Italye fast by
Dooth stand, and myndest too sayl with speede to that
     hauen :
With draw thy iudgment from that grosse cosmical erroure.
Italy is hence parted by long crosse dangerus inpaths.
In flud Trinacrian thy great oars must deeplye be bathed,
And the sea rough wurcking must eeke with nauye be trauerst,
And Circes Island se ye must with Limbo lake hellish :
Ere ye shal in saulf land of a nobil cittye be founder.
Glaunce I wyl at certeyn tokens, be ye watch ful in harckning.
When ye shal in secret with care neere fresh water happen,
Too spye bye thee banck syeds a strange sow mightelye sized,

Coompased al roundly with sucklings thirtye to number,
White, with lillye colours fayre dect, shee shal be reposed
On ground, dug dieting her mylckwhit farroed hoglings.
Heere shal cease thye labours : heere shal thy cittye be
    buylded.
Feare not thee manging fortold of burdseat in hunger,
Thee fats thee passage shal smooth, yea goulden Apollo,
If ye wyl hym summon, shal bee too the furth readye
    coomming.
But this neere setled country (that of Italy is holden
Parcel) see ye shun yt : for theare Greeks yreful are harbourd.
Heere the man of Locrus mounted steepe statelye the town-
    wals,
And fields of Salent with trouping clustered armye
Lyctius Idomeneus dooth keepe : so duke Melibæus
Holds thee prittye Petil round coompast strong bye Philoctect.
Also when in saulfty from seas thy nauye shal harboure,
When rites relligious thow vowest on new shaped altars,
With purple vesture bee deckt, with purpil eke hooded,
Least that in aduauncing thee Gods with fyrye cole heating,
Soom dismal visadge foorth peake thee mysterye marring.
Thow with thy feloes obserue this customed order.
And bye thye posterytee let theese rites duelye be foostred.
With winds neere to Sicil when that thy nauye shal enter,
And strayts shal be opned neere craggy vnweildye Pelorus,
With lifthand sayling to the liftsyde countrye be packing :
What stands on right syde both land and channel abandon.
Theese shoars were sundred by the plash breache, fame so
    doth vtter,
(So things transitory by lengthned season ar eaten)
For when theese countryes were grapled ioinctlye to geather,
Swift the sea with plasshing rusht in, townes terreblye
    drenching,
Italye disioyncting with short streicts from Sicil Island,
Scylla doth on right syde rough stand, and deadlye Charybdis
On left hand swelleth with broad iaws greedelye galping,

In to gut vpsouping three tymes thee flash water angrye,
From paunch alsoe spuing toe the sky the plash hastlye
    reccaued.
But Scylla in cabbans with sneaking treacherye lurcketh,
Close and slilye spying, too flirt thee nauye to rock bane.
A man in her visadge, then a virgin fayre she resembleth
Downe to her gastlye nauel, lyke a whale from thee belye
    seeming.
Monsterus, vnseemely, then a tayle lyke a dolphin is added
Iumbled vp of sauadge fel woulfs, with grislye lol hanging.
It wyl bee saulfer too passe thee countrye Pachynus,
With leasure lingring, and far streicts crabbye to circle,
Than to be surprised by Scylla in dungeon hellish.
Whear curs barck bawling, with yolp yalpe snarrye rebounding.
Also yf king Helenus bee now for a truprophet holden,
If fayth bee resiaunt, yf trouth to hym graunteth Apollo:
Thow soon of heunlye Godesse, this poinct I chieflye shal vtter,
And besyde al warnings eftsoons yt must be repeated:
Let Iunoes deitee with duitye be woorshiped humble.
Vnto her frame thy prayers, let mystresse mightye be
    vanquisht
With meekned presents, and then lyke a conqueror happye
From land Trinacrian thow shalt bee to Italye posted.
When ye in this passadge too Cumas cittye shall enter,
And lake with rumbling forrest of sacred Auerna,
A braynsick prophetesse se ye shal, whom dungeon holdeth
In ground deepe riueted, future haps and destenye chaunting.
But yeet al her prophecyes in greene leaues nicelye be scribled,
In theese slipprye leaues what sooth thee virgin auerreth,
Shee frams in Poëtry: her verses in dungeon howsing,
They keepe rancks ordred, with aray first setled abyding:
But when on a suddeyn thee doors winds blastye doe batter,
And theese leaues greenish with whisking lightlye be scatterd,
Neauer dooth she laboure to reuoke her flittered issue,
Or to place in cabban, theire floane lyms freshlye reioyning.
Thus they fle, detesting thee lodge of giddye Sibylla:

Heere for a spirt linger, no good opportunitye scaping.
(Al thogh thee to seaward thy posting coompanye calleth,
And winds vaunce fully thy sayls with prosperus huffing)
Post to this prophetesse, let her help and sooth be required.
Shee wyl geeue notice to the streight of al Italye dwellers :
How thow wiselye trauayls shalt shun, shalt manfulye suffer.
Theare she wyl enstruct thee, thy passadge fortunat ayding.
Theese be such od caueats, as I to the frendlye can vtter.
Foorth : and with thy valor let Troian glorye be mounted.
    When this Princely prophet this counsayl faythful had
        eended,
He wyls that presents of gould, ful weightelye poysing,
Bee broght to our vessels, and therewith eke iuorye pullisht :
Plentye great of siluer with plate most sumptuus adding.
And a shirt mayled with gould, with acrested vp helmet.
Latelye Neoptolemus possest this martial armoure.
My father Anchises rich presents alsoe receaueth.
Horses eke and captayns are sent.
And oars to oure vessels bee broght and weapon abundante.
Thee whilst Anchises wyls that thee nauye be launched,
Least that in oure loytring oure passadge lucky wer hindred.
Hym prophet of Phœbus dooth treat with dignitye peerelesse.
    Anchises, whom statelye Venus tak's woorthye for
        husband,
Thee charge of deitee, now twise from Troy ruin haled,
Italye see yoonder : thither with nauye be squdding.
How beyt theese parcels in sayling must be refused ;
Seeke the far and distant country declard of Apollo.
Fare ye wel, happye parent of a soon so worthye ; what
        oght els
Should I say ? what maks mee this gale so fortunat hynder ?
    Also good Andromachee, with last departur al heauye,
Presented vestures of gould most ritchlye bebroyded.
And my lad Ascanius with a Troian mantel adorning,
Weau'd wurcks thwackt with honor, to her gifts this parlye
        she lincketh.

Take, myeboy, theese tokens by myn owne hands finnished
    holye.
Let these of Andromachee thee good wyl testifye lasting.
Cherrish theese presents by the pheere to the tendred of
    Hector.
O next Astianax thee type by me chieflye belooued,
In visadge, looking, eke in hands thee fullye resembling.
Who had ben, yf hee liued, for yeers now youthlye thine
    equal.
    I for a long farewel this sonnet sorroful vttred.
Rest ye stil heere blessed, that now youre fortun haue
    eended :
Wee to future mischiefe from formoure danger ar hurled.
You rest in fre quiet, thee seas you need not vpharrow.
You reck not, to trauayle, that back goeth, Italye serching.
Heere the image of Zanthus ye behold, and prittye Troy
    buylded
By youre Princelye labours, and too this new shaped engyn
Thee Gods send fortune, fro assaultes too fortifye Greekish.
If that I too Tybris with necre but countrye shal enter,
And that I shal fortune to behold thee towne by me founded :
Italye with the Epeire, too both king Dardanus author,
Shal be knit in freendship, making of two pepil one Troy.
This leage eke of felo ship shalbee maynteyned of issue.
    Foorth we goa too the seaward, wee sayle bye Ceraunia
    swiftly.
Wheare too ioynctlye mearing a cantel of Italye neereth.
Thee whilste thee sunbeams are maskt, hyls darcklye be
    muffled :
Wee be put hard ioygning to the boosom of countrye
    requyred.
Oure selfs wee cherisht, oure members slumber atached.
Nor yeet was mydnight ouerhyed, when that Palinurus,
From bed nimblye fleeth, too se in what quarter yt huffeth :
How stands thee wind blast, with listning tentiue he marcketh,
Thee lights starrye noting in globe celestial hanging :

Thee seun stars stormy, twise told thee plowstar, eke
    Arcture,
Also sad Orion, with goulden flachet, in armoure.
When that he perceaued, thee coast to be cleere, then he
    summond
Oure men too ship boord, thee camp wee swiftlye remooued.
Foorth we take oure passadge, oure sayles ful winged vp
    hoysting.
Thee stars are darckned, glittring Aurora reshined.
Wee doe se swart mountayns, we doe gaze eke at Italye
    dymmed.
Italye loa yoonder, first, Italye, showted Achates.
Italye land naming, lykewise thee coompanye greeted.
Then father Anchises a goold boul massye becrowning,
With wyne brym charged, thee Gods celestial hayleth,
In ship thus speaking.
    You Gods, of sayling, of land stats mightye remayning,
Graunt to vs milde passadge, and tempest mollifye roughning.
    Sweete gales are breathing, and porte neere seated apeereth:
In the typ of mountayne thee temple of hautye Minerua
Glad we spye : thee mariners strike sayles, and roa to the
    shoareward.
The hauen from the eastcoast, in bowewise, crooked apereth.
Thee rocks sternelye facing with salt fluds spumye be
    drumming.
Downe the road is lurcking, yeet two peers loftye run vpward
From stoans lyke turrets : fro the shoare thee tempil
    auoydeth.
Heere for a first omen fowre fayre steeds snow whit I
    marcked,
Thee pasture shredding in fields ; this countrye doth offer,
Quod father Anchises, garboyls, so doe signifye war steeds.
Yeet stay : the self horses in waynes erst ioinctlye were
    hooked,
At yoked, and matchlyke teamed with common agreement.
This loa, quod hee bringeth firme hoape for peaceable vsadge.

Then we honored Pallas, that graunted a luckye beginning :
Also before the altars oure heads with purpil ar hooded,
In Troy rites, Helenus faythful direction holding.
And with setled honor thee Greekish Iuno we woorshipt.
Heere we doe not lynger; thee vowd sollemnitye finnisht,
Vp we gad, owt spredding oure sayls and make to the
    seaward :
Al creeks mistrustful with Greekish countrye refusing.
Hercules his dwelling (yf bruite bee truelye reported)
Wee se, Tarent named, to which heunlye Lacinia fronteth,
And Caulons castels we doe spy, with Scylla the wreckmake.
Then far of vplandish we doe view thee fird Sicil Ætna.
And a seabelch grounting on rough rocks rapfulye frapping
Was hard; with ramping bounce clapping neer to the seacoast
Fierce the waters ruffle, thee sands with wroght flud ar
    hoysed.
    Quod father Anchises, heere loa that scuruye Charybdis.
Theese stoans king Helenus, theese ragd rocks rustye fore
    vttred.
Hence hye, my deere feloes, duck the oars, and stick to the
    tacklings.
    Thus sayd he, then swiftly this his heast thee coompanye
        practise.
First thee pilot Palinure thee steerd ship wrigs to the lifthand,
Right so to thee same boord thee maysters al wrye the vessels.
Vp we fle too skyward with wild fluds hautye, then vnder
Wee duck too bottom with waues contrarye repressed.
Thus thrise in oure diuing thee rocks moste horribly roared :
And thrise in oure mounting to the stars thee surges vs
    heaued.
Thee winds and soonbeams vs, poore souls weerye, refused,
And to soyl of Cyclops with wandring iournye we roamed.
A large roade fenced from rough ventositye blustring.
    But neere ioynctlye brayeth with rufflerye rumboled Ætna.
Soomtyme owt yt balcketh from bulck clowds grimlye
    bedymmed.

Lyke fyerd pitche skorching, or flash flame sulphurus heating:
Flownce to the stars towring thee fire, lyke a pellet, is hurled,
Ragd rocks vp raking: and guts of mounten yrented
From roote vp hee iogleth: stoans hudge slag molten he
    rowseth:
With route snort grumbling, in bottom flash furye kendling.
Men say that Enceladus with bolt haulf blasted here
    harbrouth,
Dingd with this squising and massiue burthen of Ætna,
Which pres on hym nayled from broached chymnye stil
    heateth.
As oft as the giant his broyld syds croompeled altreth,
So oft Sicil al shiuereth, there with flaks smoakye be
    sparckled.
    That night in forrest to vs pouke bugs gastlye be tendred.
Thee cause wee find not, for noise phantastical offred.
Thee stars imparted no light, thee welken is heauye:
And the moon enshryned with closet clowdye remayned.
    Thee morning brightnesse dooth luster in east seat Eöus,
And night shades moysturs glittring Aurora repealeth.
When that on a suddeyn we behold a windbeaten hard
    shrimp,
With lanck wan visadge, with rags iags patcherye clowted,
His fists too the skyward rearing: heere wee stood amazed.
A meigre leane rake with a long berd goatlyke; aparrayld
In shrub weeds thorny: by his byrth a Grecian holden.
One that too Troy broyls whillon from his countrye repayred.
When the skrag had marcked far a loof thee Troian atyring,
And Troian weapons, in steps he stutted, apaled:
And fixt his footing, at leingth with desperat offer
Too the shore hee neered, theese speeches merciful vttring.
    By stars I craue you, by the ayre, by the celical houshold,
Hoyse me hence (O Troians) too sum oother countrye me
    whirrye.
Playnelye to speake algats, for a Greeke my self I doe
    knowledge,

And that I too Troytowne with purposed emnitye sayled.

If this my trespasse now claymeth duelye reuengment

Plunge me deepe in the waters, and lodge me in Neptun his harboure.

If mens hands slea mee, such mannish slaughter I wish for.

  Thus sayd he, downe kneeling, and oure feete mournefuly clasping.

Then we hym desyred first too discoouer his ofspring,

After too manifest this his hard and destenye bitter.

My father Anchises gaue his hand to the wretch on a suddeyn,

And with al a pardon, with saulfe protection, offred.

Thee captiue, shaking of feare, too parlye thus entred.

  Borne I was in the Itacan countrey, mate of haples Vlisses,

Named Achæmenides, my syre also cald Adamastus,

A good honest poore man (would we in that penurye lasted)

Sent me toe your Troywars, at last my coompanye skared

From this countrye cruel, dyd posting leaue me behynde theym,

In Cyclops kennel, thee laystow dirtye, the foule den.

In this grislye palaice, in forme and quantitye mightye,

Palpable and groaping darcknesse with murder aboundeth.

Hee doth in al mischiefe surpasse, hee mounts to the sky top.

(Al the heunly feloship from the earth such a monster abandon)

Hard he is too be viewed, too se hym no person abydeth.

Thee blud with the entrayls of men, by hym slaughtred, he gnaweth.

And of my feloes I saw that a couple he grapled

On ground sow grooueling, and theym with villenye crusshed,

At flint hard dasshing, thee goare blood spowteth of eeche syde,

And swyms in the thrashold, I saw flesh bluddye toe slauer,

When the cob had maunged the gobets foule garbaged haulfe quick.

Yeet got he not shotfree, this butcherye quighted Vlisses:

In which doughtye peril the Ithacan moste wiselye bethoght hym.

For the vnsauerye rakhel with collops bludred yfrancked,

With chuffe chaffe wynesops lyke a gourd bourrachoe
    replennisht,
His nodil in crossewise wresting downe droups to the
    growndward,
In belche galp vometing with dead sleape snortye the collops,
Raw with wyne soused, we doe pray toe supernal asemblye,
Round with al embaying thee muffe maffe loller; eke hastlye
With toole sharp poincted wee boarde and perced his oane
        light,
That stood in his lowring front gloommish malleted onlye.
Lyke Greekish tergat glistring, or Phœbus his hornebeams.
Thus the death of feloes on a lout wee gladlye reuenged.
But se ye flee caytiefs, hy ye hence, cut swiftlye the cables.
Pack fro the shoare.
For such as in prison thee great Polyphemus is holden,
His sheepflocks foddring, from dugs mylck thriftelye squising,
Thee lyke heere in mountayns doo randge in number an
        hundred,
That bee cursd Cyclopes in naming vsual highted.
Thee moone three seasons her passadge orbical eended
Sence I heere in forrest and cabbans gastlye dyd harboure,
With bestes fel saluadge: and in caues stoanye Cyclopes
Dayly I se, theire trampling and yelling hellish abhorring.
My self I dieted with sloas, and thinlye with hawthorns,
With mast, and with roots of eeche herb I swadgde my great
        hunger.
I pryed al quarters, and first this nauye to shoare ward
Swift, I scryed, sayling too which my self I remitted,
Of what condicion, what countryso eauer yt had beene.
Now tis sufficient that I skape fro this horribil Island.
Mee rather extinguish with soom blud murther or oother.
    Scant had he thus spoaken: when that from mountenus
        hil toppe
Al wee see the giaunt, with his hole flock lowbylyke hagling.
Namde the shepeherd Polyphem, to the wel knowne sea syd
        aproching.

A fowle fog monster, great swad, depriued of eyesight.
His fists and stalcking are propt with trunck of a pynetree.
His flock hym doe folow, this charge hym chiefly reioyceth.
In grief al his coomfort on neck his whistle is hanged.
When that too the seasyde thee swayne Longolius hobbled,
Hee rinst in the water thee drosse from his late bored
  eyelyd.
His tusk grimlye gnashing, in seas far waltred, he groyleth:
Scantly doo the water surmounting reache toe the shoulders.
But we being feared, from that coast hastlye remooued,
And with vs embarcked thee Greekish suitur, as amplye
His due request merited, wee chopt of softlye the cables.
Swift wee sweepe the seafroth with nimble lustilad oare
  striefe.
Thee noise he perceaued, then he turning warelye listeth,
But when he considerd, that wee preuented his handling,
And that from foloing oure ships thee fluds hye reuockt hym,
Loud the lowbye brayed with belling monsterus eccho:
Thee water hee shaketh, with his owt cryes Italye trembleth.
And with a thick thundring thee fyerde fordge Ætna
  rebounded.
Then runs from mountayns and woods thee rownseual
  helswarme
Of Cyclopan lurdens to the shoars in coompanye clustring.
Far we se theym distaunt: vs grimly and vaynely beholding.
Vp to the sky reatching, thee breetherne swish swash of Ætna.
A folck moaste fulsoom, for sight moste fitlye resembling
Trees of loftye cipers, with thickned multitud oakroas:
Or Ioues great forrest, or woods of mightye Diana.
Feare thear vs enforced with posting speedines headlong
Too swap of oure cables, and fal to the seas at auenture.
But yeet king Helenus iumptwixt Scylla and the Charybdis
For to sayl vs monished, with no great dangerus hazard.
Yeet we wer ons mynded, backward thee nauye to mayster.
Heere loa behold Boreas from bouch of north blo Pelorus
Oure ships ful chargeth, thee quick rocks stoanye we passed:

And great Pantagia, and Megarus with Tapsus his Island.
Theese soyls fore wandred to oure men were truelye related
By poore Achæmenides, mate too thee luckles Vlisses.
Face too countrye Sicil theare stands a dangerus Island.
Plemmyrium stormy, but yt old past auncetrye cleaped
Ortygia : Alpheüs, men say, thee great flud of Elis
Vnder seabottoms this passadge ferreted, and now
Swift fro Arethusa going meets in fluds of Sicil Island.
That country deitee, thogh wild, wee woorshiped, and thence
Wee sayld and trauayled to the coast of fertil Elorus.
Then we grate on rockrayes and bancks of stoanye Pachynus,
And Camarina riuer, to remooue by destenye barred.
Also we through passed thee fields of statelye Geloüs,
And thee mightye water, by custoom great Gela named.
Thence strong buylt Agragas his huge high wals loftelye
        vaunceth,
That steeds courrageous with racebrood plentiful offred.
And with lyke sayling wee passe thee wooddye Selinis :
And deepe gulfs syncking of blind Lilybeia rockish.
After too Drepanus bad roade not luckye we sayled.
Heere loa being scaped from rough tempestuus huffling,
My father Anchises, in cares my accustomed helper,
I loose : ô my father, wyl you forsake me, thus eending
My toyls and my trauayls, why then dyd I mayster al hazards?
Nor propheting Helenus, when he foretold dangerus hard
        haps
Forspake this burial mourning, nor filthye Celæno.
This was last my laboure, thee knot claspt of myn auentures.
From hence God me shoou'd too this your gratius empyre.
    Thus father Æneas soly toe the coompanye listning
His long dryrye viadge, and Gods set destenye chaunted.
At leingth kept he silence, with finnished historye resting.

Finis libri tertij.

THEE FOVRTH
BOOKE OF VIR-
GIL HIS ÆNEIS.

Vt the Queene in meane while with carks
    quandare deepe anguisht,
Her wound fed by Venus, with firebayt
    smoldred is hooked.
Thee wights doughtye manhood leagd with
    gentilytye nobil,
His woords fitlye placed, with his heunly
    phisnomye pleasing,
March throgh her hert mustring, al in her brest deepelye she
    printeth.
Theese carcking cratchets her sleeping natural hynder.
Thee next day foloing Phœbus dyd clarifye brightlye
Thee world with luster, watrye shaads Aurora remooued,
When to her deere sister, with woords, haulf gyddye she
    raueth.
    Sister An, I merueyle, what dreams mee terrefye napping,
What newcoom trauayler, what guest in my harborye
    lighted ?
How braue he dooth court yt ? what strength and coorrage
    he carryes ?
I beleue yt certeyn (ne yet hold I yt vaynelye reported)
That fro the great linnadge of Gods his pettegre shooteth.

Feare shews pitfle crauens : good God, what destenye way-
ward
Hath the man endured ? what bickrings bitter he passed ?
Had not I foresnaffled my mynde by votarye promise,
Not toe yoke in wedlock too no wight earthlye mye person,
When my first feloship by murther beastlye was eended,
Had not I such daliaunce, such pipling bedgle renounced,
Haplye this oane faulty trespas might bring me toe bending.
An (toe the my meaning and mynd I doe playnelye set open)
Sence the death of my husband, too wyt, the Sichæus
vnhappye,
Sence mye cruel broother defilde the domestical altars :
Onlye this od gallant hath bowd my phansye toe lyking,
And my looue hath gayned : thee skorcht step of old fyre I
sauoure.
But first with vengaunce let the earth mee swallo toe
bottom,
Or father omnipotent with lightnings dyng me toe lymbo,
And to Erebus shading darcknesse, too dungeon hellish,
Eare that I shal thye statutes (ô shamefast chastitye) cancel.
Hee, that first me yoked for wiefe, dyd carrye my first looue,
Hardlye let hym shrowd yt, close claspt in graue let yt
harboure.
When she thus had spoaken, with tears her brest she
replennisht.
    Then sayd An (ô sister, than light more deerely belooued)
Wyl ye stil in pining youre youthful ioylitye stiefle ?
Wyl ye not haue children, nor sweete Venus happye
rewarding's ?
Weene ye that oure lyking a scalp of a charuel In heedeth ?
Graunt, earst that noe woer could catche youre phansye to
wedlock,
Nor Lybye land lordinges, ne by Tyre despised Iärbas,
Nor manye stat's lofty, that rest in plentiful Affrick :
Wyl ye stil endeuoure with pleasd looue vaynelye to iustle ?
Wyl ye be forgetting in what curst countrye ye soiourne ?

Heere towns of Getuls doo stand, a nation hardye,

Heere ye sit embayed with Moors, with Syrtis vnhowsed.

Theare pepil of Barcey through soale wyld barrenes harboure.

What shal I tel further, what broyle Tyrus angrye doth
  hammer.

What threats your broother thunders.

I thinck, that the Godhead, with Iunoes prosperus ayding,

Thee Troian vessels too this youre segnorye pelted.

Loa what a fayre citty shal mount, what stablished empyre

By this great wedlock : with might of the vnitye Troian.

How far shal be fleing thee glorie renowmed of Affrick.

Of Gods craue pardon, then, when your seruice is eended,

Your new guest frollick, his stay let forgerye linger,

Til winters lowring bee past, and rayne make Orion.

Til they rig al vessels, vntil tyme stormye be swaged.

  With theese woords flaming her brest was kendled in
    hoatlooue :

Shee graunts to her tottring mynd hoape, shame bashful
    auoyding.

First to the church gad they, rest and peace meekelye
    requesting,

In sacrifice killing, by woont accustomed, hogrels :

First to Ceres makelaw, too Phœbus, then to Lyæus :

Chieflye to Queene Iuno, that wedlocks vnitye knitteth.

Thee bol in hand firmely Queene Dido, the bewtiful, holding,

Pourd yt a mydst both the horns peaking of lillye white heyfer.

Soomtyme to the altars, distant, of Gods she resorteth :

And makes fresh sacrifice, the catal, new slaughtered,
    heeding.

Shee weens her fortune by guts, hoate smoakye, to conster.

ó the superstitions of beldam trumperye sooth says.

Now what auayle temples, or vows, whilst deepelye the
    flamd fire

Kendleth in her marrow, whilst wound in brest cel is aking.

Dido, the wretch, burneth, neere mad through cittye she
    stalketh :

Much lyke a doa wounded too death, not marcked of heerd-
    man,
His dart sharp headed through forrest Cassian hurling,
On the doa iump lighteth by soom chaunce medlye : the
    weapon,
Thee bodye sore ranckling dooth stur thee deere to the
    frithward,
Or to falow straining, in corps thee deadly staf hangeth.
    Often about thee wals Æneas slilye she trayneth :
Too welth Sidonian poincting, too cittye nere eended.
Her bye tale owt hauking amyd oft her parlye she chocketh.
Soomtyme she inuites theym too deynty bancquet in
    eeuening :
Now fresh agayne crauing of Troian toyle the recital,
From lyps of Chronicler with blincking listenes hanging.
When they be departed, when light of mooneshine is housed,
And stars downe gliding at due tyme of slumber ar ayming,
Restles aloane sobbing on left benche soalye she sytteth :
Her selfe not present she both hyers and sees the man absent,
Or the slip Ascanius (for sainct thee shrinecase adoring)
Shee cols for the father : with busse to lenifye loouefits.
Thee towrs new founded mount not, thee coompanye
    youthful
Surcease from warfeats, there toyls no swincker in hauen ;
Nor mason in bulwarck : wurcks interrupted ar hanging.
And wals hudge menacing, thee sky top in altitud eeuening.
When the plage of pacient thee spouse of Iuppiter heeded,
And noe reporte wandring thee looue furye kendled abated,
Thus toe Venus turning spake thee Saturnical empresse.
    A praise of high reckning, eke a catche to be greatlye
    renowmed
You with youre pricket purchast, loa the victorye famouse :
With two Gods packing one woomman sellye to coosen.
Wel dyd I know, mistresse, that you my great harborye
    feared,
Mightelye mistrusting thee seats of Carthage, hye mounted.

When shal, Hoa, bee shouted ? too what drift feede we this
anger ?
Why be we not forward theese mat's too marrye to geather
And a leage eternal conclude ? thy long wish is hested.
Dido with hertlyking dooth burne, her boans furye fretteth.
Let theese sundrye pepils theare for bee lincked in one loare.
Also let oure Dido vayle her hert too bedfeloe Troian :
And Tyrian kingdooms to the shal, for dowrye, be graunted.
    Then to her (for wisely shee found thee treacherye feined
Too fetch too Tyrians the great empyre of Italye woorcking)
Thus Venus her speeches dyd bend. What niddipol hare
brayne
Would scorne this couenaunt ? would with thee gladlye be
iarring ?
If so this happye trauayle shal so be with happines ayded.
But fates mee stamering doo make, yf Iuppiter holdeth
Best, that the Tyrians and Troian progenye couple,
That they be conioigned, that both they freendlye be leaged.
You to hym bee spoused : thee trouth with pillotoy ferret.
On before, and I folow.   Too this ladye Iuno replyed.
    That labor I warrant.   Now by what craftinis are wee
Too wurck this stratagem : marck wel, for I brieflye wyl open.
Thee Prince Æneas and eke Queene Dido the poore soule
For to hunt in forrest too morro be fullye resolued.
So soon as in east coaste with bright beams Titan apeereth.
Then wyl I round coompasse with clowd grim foggye these
hunters.
When they shal in thickets thee coouert maynelye be
drawing.
Al the skye shal rustle with thumping thunderus hurring.
Thee men I wyl scatter, they shal be in darcknes al hooueld.
Dido and thee Troian captayne shal iumble in one den.
If with this my trauayle thy mynd and phansye be meeting
Then wyl I thee wedlock with firme affinitye fasten :
This shal bee the bryde hymne. To the drift Venus, vttred,
agreed,

Smoothlye with al simpring, too groape suche treacherus
    handling.
    Thee whilst thee dawning Aurora fro the Ocean hastned,
And the May fresh yoonckers to the gates doo make there
    assemblye
With nets and catch toyls, and huntspears plentiful yrond :
With the hounds quicksenting, with pricking galloper
    horsman.
Long for thee Princesse thee Moors gentilitye wayted,
As yet in her pincking not pranckt with trinckerye trinckets :
As they stood attending thee whilst her trapt genet hautye
Deckt with ritche scarlet, with gould stood furniture
    hanging,
Praunseth on al startling, and on byt gingled he chaumpeth.
At leingth foorth she fleeth with swarming coompanye circled,
In cloke Sidonical with rich dye brightlye besprinckled.
Her locks are broyded with gould, her quiuer is hanging
Backward : with gould tache thee vesture purple is holden.
Thee band of Troians lykewise, with wanton Iülus
Doo marche on forward : but of al thee Lucifer heunlye
In bewty Æneas hymself to the coompanye rancketh.
Lyke when as hard frozen Lycia and Zanth floods be
    relinquisht
By Pheebe, to Delos, his natiue contrye seat, hastning.
Hee poinctes a dawnsing, foorth with thee rustical hoblobs
Of Cretes, of Dryopes, and payncted clowns Agathyrsi
Dooe fetch theyre gambalds hopping neere consecrat altars.
Hee trips on Zanthus mountayn, with delicat hearelocks
Trayling : with greene shrubs and pure gould neatly be-
    crampound
His shafts on shoulder rattle : the lyke hautye resemblaunce
Carried Æneas with glistring coomlines heunlye.
    When they toe thee mountayns and too layrs vncoth
    aproched,
Then, loa, behold ye, breaking thee goats doo trip fro the
    rocktops

Neere toe the playne : the heard deare dooth stray from
    mounten vnharbourd.
Thee chase is ensued with passadge dustye bepowdred.
But the lad Ascanius, with praunsing courser hye mounted,
Dooth manage in valley, now theym, now theese ouer-
    ambling.
Hee scornes theese rascal tame games, but a sounder of
    hogsteers,
Or thee brownye lion too stalck fro the mounten he wissheth.
    Thee whilst in the skye seat great bouncing rumbelo
      thundring
Ratleth : downe powring too sleete thick hayle knob is added.
Thee Tyrian feloship with yoouthful Troian assemblye
And Venus hautye nephew doo run too sundrye set houses.
Hudge fluds lowdlye freaming from mountayns loftye be
    trowlling,
Dido and thee Troian captayne doo iumble in one den.
Then the earth crau's the banes, theare too watrye Iuno, the
    chaplayne,
Seams vp thee bedmatch, the fyre and ayre testifie wedlock.
And Nymphs in mountayns high typ doe squeak, hullelo,
    yearning :
That day cros and dismal was cause of mischief al after,
And bane of her killing ; her fame for sleight she regarded.
No more dooth she laboure too mask her Phansye with
    hudwinck,
With thee name of wedlock her carnal leacherye cloaking,
Straight through towns Lybical this fame with an infamye
    rangeth.
    Fame the groyl vngentil, then whom none swifter is
      extant ;
Limber in her whisking : her streingth in iournye she
    trebbleth ;
First lyke a shrimp squatting for feare, then boldlye she
    roameth
On ground prowd ietting : shee soars vp nimblye toe skyward ;

The earth, her dame, chauffing with graund Gods celical
    anger,
Litterd this leueret, the syb, as men sundrye rehersed,
Too the giant Cæus, sister to swad Encelad holden.
Furth she quicklye galops, with wingflight swallolyke
    hastning.
A foule fog pack paunch: what feathers plumye she beareth,
So manye squint eyebals shee keeps (a relation vncoth)
So manye tongues clapper, with her ears and lip labor
    eeuened.
In the dead of nighttyme to the skyes shee flickereth, howling
Through the earth shade skipping, her sight from slumber
    amoouing.
Whilst the sun is shyning the bagage close lodgeth in
    housroofs,
Or tops of turrets, with feare towns loftye she frighteth.
As readye forgde fittons, as true tales vaynelye toe twattle.
Thee pepil in iangling this raynebeaten harlotrye filled:
Meerelye furth chatting feats past, and feats not atempted.
That the duke Æneas from Troians auncetrye sprouting,
In Lybye coast landed, with whom fayre Dido, the Princesse,
Her person barterd, and that they both be resolued,
Thee winter season too wast in leacherye wanton.
Retchles of her kingdom, with rutting bitcherye sauted.
This that prat'pye cadesse labored too trumpet in eeche
    place.
    Furth she fleeth posting to the kingly rector Iarbas.
With the brute enflaming his mynd she doth huddle on
    anger.
Soon to the Prince Ammon, Garamans thee fayrye, bye
    rapesnacht,
His moother named; this king too Iuppiter heunly
Temples twise fifty dyd buyld, lyke number of altars,
With fire continual theese seats too consecrat vsing,
With the blud of sacrifice floating, with delicat herbflowrs.
Netled with theese brackye nouels as wild as a marche hare

In the myd of the Idols (men tel) neere furnished altars,
Theese woords, vplifting both his hands, he toe Iuppiter
vttred.
   Iuppiter almighty, whom men Maurusian, eating
On the tabils vernisht, with cuprit's magnifye dulye :
Eyest thow this filthood ? shal wee, father heunlye, be
carelesse
Of thy claps thundring ? or when fiers glimrye be listed
In clowds grim gloomming with bounce doo terrifye
worldlings ?
A coy tyb, as vagabund in this my segnorye wandring,
That the plat of Carthage from mee by coosinage hooked,
T'whom gaue I fayre tilladge, and eeke lawes needful enacted,
Hath scornd my wedlock : Æneas lord she reteyneth.
Now this smocktoy Paris with berdlesse coompanye wayted,
With Greekish coronet, with falling woommanish hearelocks
Lyke fiest hound mylcksop trimd vp, thee victorye catcheth.
And wee beat the bushes, thee stil with woorship adoring.
Onlye for oure seruice soom praysed vanitye gleaming.
   Thee prayer of playntiefe, grappling thee consecrat altars,
Iuppiter hard ; foorth with to, the courte hee whirled his
eyesight,
And viewd theese bedmat's no sound reputation heeding.
With woords imperial thus he speaks and Mercurye chargeth.
   Flee my sun, and busk on, let sweete winds swiftlye be
soommond,
And toe the duke Troian, that vaynelye in Carthage abydeth,
Thee towns neglecting, that to hym set destenye lotteth,
Theese woords deliuer, from mee to hym carrye this errand.
His paragon moother to vs framd a promise of hudgger
Accoumpt and reckning, then he now perfourmeth, vpon that
Hoape future expected, from Troy flam's twise she reliu'd
hym.
Too me she dyd promise, that he should bee the emperor
hautye,
That would, with bickring, fierce martial Italye vanquish :

Thee Troian famely with wide spread glorye reuiuing :
And globe of al regions with laws right equitye bridle.
Too feats so valiant yf that no glorye doth hasthym,
Or to hym thee catching of fame so woorthye be toyle soom :
Shal, by syre, Ascanius from Roman cittye be loytred ?
What doth he forge ? wherefore wil he rest in countrye so
    freendlesse ?
Why the Lauin regions, and stock, he so slilye reputeth ?
Thee sea let hym trauerse : this is al : to hym signifye this
    muche.
  Ioue sayd : eke hee the fathers commaund to accomplisse
    apoincteth.
First of al his woorcking too his feete shooes goulden he
    knitteth,
By which he with wind blast ruffling oft flittereth vpward,
Wheather he land regions or rough seas surgye doth harrow.
His rod next he handleth : by which from the helly Bocardo
Touzt tost souls he freeth : diuerse to the prison he plungeth.
Hee causeth sleeping and bars : bye death eyelyd vphasping.
With the rod eke he sheareth thee winds, and scattereth high
    clowds.
As thus he dyd flicker, thee top wyth sideryb of Atlas
He sees, that proppeth, with crowne, the supernal Olympus,
Atlas, whose pallet with pynetrees plentiful hooueld,
In grim clowds darckned, with showrs and windpuf is haunted.
Thee snoa whit his shoulders dooth cloath, fluds mightye be
    rowling
From the chyn oldlye riueld, his beard with froast hoare is
    hardned.
First on this mounteyn thee winged Mercurie lighted :
From thence too the waters his course hee bended al
    headlong.
Muche lyke a byrd nestled neere shoars or desolat hilrocks :
Not to the sky maynely, but neere sea meanelye she flickreth.
So with a meane passadge twixt sky and sea Mercurye
    slideth

To Lyby coast sandy; thee sharp wynds speedelye shauing,
Mercurye thee Cyllen, bye the mount Cyllene begotten.
On Lyby land tenements with winged feete when he lighted,
Hee spyed Æneas new castels thriftelye founding,
And howsrowms altring: hee woare then a gorgeus hanger
With iaspar yellow: hee shynde with mantel ypurpled,
From shoulders trayling: this braue roabe Dido, the ritch
  Queene,
Soalye with her handwurck dyd weaue: with gould wyre yt
  heaping.
  Mercurye thus greets hym: Now sir, you wholye be carefull
Too found new Carthage, with youre braue bedfelo sotted
You buyld a cittye, youre owne state slilye regarding.
Now to the God sentmee from shining brightned Olympus,
The God of al the godheads, managing heune and places
  earthlye,
Hee gaue commaundement, too thee too carrye this erraund.
What doe ye forge? wherefore thus vaynely in land Lybye
  mitche you?
Too feats ful valiant yf that no glorye doth egge the,
Or toe the thee catching of fame soo woorthye be toyl soom,
Cast care on Ascanius rising, of the heyrs of Iülus.
Tw'hom the stat Italian with Roman cittye belongeth.
  When this round message thee Cyllen Mercurye whisperd,
In myd of his parling from gazing mortal he shrincketh:
From lookers eyesight too thinnes he vannished ayrye.
  But the duke Æneas with sight so geason agasted,
His bush starck staring with feare, cleene speecheles abyded.
Hee to fle soare longeth, this sweet soyl streight to relinquish,
By Gods imperial monishing auctoritye warned.
Heere but alas he myred what course may be warelye taken;
How shal he too Princesse, with looues hoat phrensye reteyned,
Breake this cold messadge? what woords shal shape the
  beginning.
From thee poast toe piler with thoght his rackt wyt he tosseth.
Now to this od stratagem, now too that counseyl alying.

After long mooting, this course for better he deemed.
Mnestheus hee called, Sergest and manlye Cloanthus,
For to rig in secret theyre ships, and coompanye summon,
With weapons ready: Thee cause also of changabil hastning
Deepelye toe dissemble : when eke opportunitye serued,
Whilst no breche of freendship thee good ladye Dido
    remembers,
And due place of speaking sweetly with season is offred,
They would theire passadge close steale. Thee knightes
    agreed,
With wil moste forward, to haste on too iournye resolued.
    How beyt thee Princesse (what wyle can iuggle a loouer?)
Found owt this cogging: in thoght what first she reuolued
That toe doe they mynded : things standing saulflye she
    feareth.
Fame, the blab vnciuil, fosters her phansye reciting,
That the fleete is strongly furnisht, their passage apoincted.
Deuoyd of al counsayle scolding through cittye she ploddeth.
Mutch lyke Dame Thyas with great sollemnitye sturred
Of Bacchus third yeers feasting, when quaftyde aproacheth,
And showts in nighttyme doo ringe in loftye Cithæron.
At last she Æneas thus, not prouoked, asaulteth.
    And thoghst thow, faythlesse coystrel, so smoothlye to
    shaddow
Thy packing practise? from my soyle priuelye slincking?
Shal not my lyking, ne yet earst fayth plighted in handclaspe,
Nor Didoes burial from this crosse iournye withold the?
Further; in a winters soure storme must nauye be launched?
Mind'st thow with northen bluster thee mayne sea to trauerse
Thow cruel hert haggard? what? yf hence too countrye the
    passage
Thow took'st not stranged : suppose Troy cittye remayned :
Through the sea fierce swelling would'st thow to Troy cittye
    be packing?
Shunst thow my presence? By theese tear's, and by thye
    right hand

(Sence that I, poore caytiefe, noght els to mye self doe
  relinquish)
By the knot of wedlock, by looues sollemnitye sealed,
If that I deserued too fore soom kindnes, or ennye
Part of my person to the whillon pleasur a furded
To my state empayring let yeet soom mercye be tenderd.
I doe craue (yf toe prayers as yeet soom nouke be reserued)
Beat downe thy purpose, thy mynd from iournye reclayming.
For thy sake in Lybical regions and in Nemod hateful
I liue: my Tyrian subiectes pursue me with anger.
For thy sake I stayned whillon my chastitye spotlesse :
And honor old batterd, to the sky with glorye me lifting.
And now, guest, wheather doe ye skud from deaths fit of
  hostace ?
That terme must I borowe, syth I dare not cal the myne
  husband.
Why do I breath longer ? shall I liue til cittye mye broother
Pigmalion ransack ? or too tyme I be prisoner holden
By thee Getul Iärb ? yf yeet soom progenye from me
Had crawld, by the fatherd, yf a cockney dandiprat
  hopthumb,
Prittye lad Æneas, in my court, wantoned, ere thow
Took'st this filthye fleing, that thee with phisnomye lyckned,
I ne then had reckned my self for desolat owtcaste.
  She sayd : he persisting too doo what Iuppiter heasted,
Sturd not an eye, graueling in his hert his sorroful anguish.
At length thus briefly dyd he parle : I may not, I wil not
Deny thy beneficts ful as amply, as can be recounted,
Vnto me deliu'red : so long shal I Dido remember,
Whilst I my self mynd shal : whilst lyms with spirit ar
  orderd.
Brieflye for a weighty matter few woords I wil vtter.
Neauer I foremynded (let not mee falslye be threpped)
For toe slip in secret by flight : ne yet eauer I thralled
My self too wedlock : I toe no such chapmenhed harckned.
If toe mye mind priuat my fatal fortun agreed.

If so that al sorrows iump with my phansye were eended,
Then should bee chiefly bye me Troian cittye redressed,
And kinreds rellicques woorshipt : then should be renewed
Thee courte of Priamus : yea thogh that victorye razed
Theese monuments, yet agayne by mee they should be
    repayred.
But now to Italian kingdooms vs sendeth Apollo,
And vs to Italian regions set destenye warneth.
Theare rests oure lyking : there eke oure wisht countrye
    remayneth.
If ye be delighted, too see new Carthage vp hoouering,
And a Moore in Morish citty youre phansye ye settle :
Why so may not Troian theire course to good Italye
    coompasse ?
What reason embars theym, soom forreyn countrye to
    ferret ?
Of father Anchises thee goast and grislye resemblaunce,
When the day dooth vannish, when lights eke starrye be
    twinckling,
In sleepe mee monisheth, with visadge buggish he feareth.
And my sun Ascanius mee pricks, by me rightlye belooued :
Whom from the Italian regions toe toe long I doe linger.
Latelye toe mee posted from Ioue thee truch sprit, or herrald
Of Gods (thee deityes this sooth too wytnes I summon)
He dyd, in expressed commaund, to me message his erraund.
I saw most liuely, when that neere towne wal he lighted ;
In this eare hee towted thee speeche. Cease therefor, I pray
    you,
Mee to teare, and also youre self, with drirye rehersals.
Italye not willing I seeke.
    Whilst he thus in pleading dyd dwel, shee surlye beheeld
    hym :
Heere she dothe her visadge, thear skew, eeche member in
    inchmeale
In long mummye silence limming : then shrewdlye she
    scoldeth.

No Godes is thye parent, nor th'wart of Dardanus ofspring,
Thow periurde faytoure: but amydst rocks, Caucasus haggish
Bred the, with a tigers soure milck vnseasoned, vdderd.
What shal I dissemble? what poincts more weightye
    reserue I?
At my tears showring dyd he sigh? dyd he winck with his
    eyelyd?
Ons dyd he weepe vanquisht? dyd he yeeld ons mercye toe
    loouemate?
What shal I first vtter? wyl not graund Iuno with hastning,
Nor thee father Saturne with his eyes bent rightlye behold-
    this?
Fayth quite is exiled: fro the shoare late a runnagat hedgebrat,
A tarbreeche quystroune dyd I take, with phrensye betrasshed
I placed in kingdoom, both ships and coompanye gracing.
Woa to me thus stamping, sutch braynsick foolerye belching.
Marck the speak, I pray you, wel coucht: Now sothtel
    Apollo,
Now Lycians fortuns, from very Iuppiter heunlye
A menacing message, by the Gods ambassador, vttred.
Foorsooth; this thye viadge with care Saincts celical heapeth,
Theire brayns vnquieted with this baldare be buzing.
I stay not thye body, ne on baw vaw tromperye descant.
Pack toe soyl Italian: crosse thee seas: fish for a kingdoom.
Verely, in hoape rest I (yf Gods may take duelye reueng-
    ment)
With gagd rocks coompast, then vaynely, Dido, reciting,
Thow shalt bee punnisht. Ile with fyre swartish hop after.
When death hath vntwined my soule from carcas his holding,
I wyl, as hobgoblin, foloa thee: thow shalt be soare handled:
I shal hyre, I doubt not, thy pangs in lymbo related.
    Her talck in the mydel, with this last parlye, she throtled.
And from his sight parted, with tortours queazye disorderd.
Hym shee left daunted with feare, woords duitiful hamring
For to reply. The lady sowning mayds carrye to smooth bed
Of marble glittring, on beers her softlye reposing.

But the good Æneas (al thogh that he cooueted hertlye,
For to swage her malady, with woords to qualifye sorrows)
In groans deepe scalding, his kindmynd sindged in hoatlooue,
Yeet the wyl of the Godheads foloing, too nauye returneth.
Thee Troian mariners now drudge: theire fleet they doe
    lavnch foorth:
And vessels, calcked with roasen smearye, be floating.
Vp they trus oars boughed with plancks vnfinnished, hastning
From thence theire passadge.
Now to the strond may ye see from towne thee multitude
    hopping.
Much lyk when pismers theire corner in granar ar hurding,
Careful of a winter nipping, in barns they be piling.
Thee blackgarde marching dooth wurck, in path way, ther
    haruest.
Parte of theese laborers on shoulders carrye the burdens
Of shocks: soom grangers with goade iads restye be pricking,
And spur on ants luskish, with swinck eeche corner
    aboundeth.
But toe the, poore Dido, this sight so skearye beholding,
What feeling creepeth? what sobbing sorroful hert sigh
In thy corps hized, when from towre, loftelye mounted,
Thow saw'st thee bancksydes coouerd, and right to thyne
    eyesight
Thow saw'st seas ringing with cheering clamorus hoyssayle?
Scuruye loue, in pacients what moods thow mightelye forcest.
Now she is constrayned, too formoure tears toe be turning.
With suit freshlye praying, too looue shee tendereth hommage.
No meane vnattempted, ne vnsoght, ear that she dye, leauing.
Sister An, in cluster you see thee coompanye swarming
On the shoare in flockmeale: for wind theire sayles ar hoysted.
On sterne thee mariners haue setled meerelye garlands.
If that I foremynded this greefe so mischeuus hapned,
Then should I, sister, moderat this sorroful hazard.
Yeet good An, I pray thee, doe me wretch this pleasure in
    one thing.

For the chiefe of woomen this breakeuow naughtyc regarded,
Chieflye to the hee wounted to recount his priuitye secret.
His daps and sweetening good moods to the soalye were
  opned.
Post to hym (good sister) toe my proud foa tel ye this
  erraund.
I dyd not ransack, with Greeks conspiracye, Troytowne.
Nor yet agaynst Troians send I enny vessel apoincted.
Nor father Anchises boans crusht I, ne scattred his ashes.
What reason hym leadeth to my suite too boombas his
  hyring?
Wheather is hee flitting? To his leefe pheere graunt he this
  one boone,
Too stay for a better passadge, for a prosperus hufgale,
I clayme no old wedlock, that he fowly and falslye betrayed.
Nor that he thee regiment doo loose of his Italye kingdooms.
I craue a vayne respit, but a spirt toe mye phrensye relenting,
Til my fate hath schoold mee too mourne my destenye
  drowping.
Theese I craue in pardon for last (yeeld mercye to sister)
Which when you tender, toe mye death that shal be
  requighted.
  In this wise she prayed : such tears her sister vnhappye
Dooth to and fro carry : but he with no tearedrop is altred :
Nor to vayne entreatings with listning tractable harckneth.
Thee fat's are pugnant, God, his ears quight stifned in
  hardnesse.
Much lyke as in forrest a long set dottrel, or oaktree,
With northen blusters too parts contrayrye retossed :
Thee winds scold strugling, the threshing thick crush crash
  is owtborne,
Thee boughs frap whurring, when stem with blastbob is
  hacked :
Yeet the tre stands sturdy : for as yt toe the skytyp is
  haunced,
So far is yt crampornd with roote deepe dibled at helgat's :

So this courragious gallant with clustered erraunds
Is cloyed and stinging sharp car's in brest doe lye thrilling.
His mynd vnuariant doth stand, tears vaynelye doe gutter.
  Dido the poore Princesse gauld with such destenye cutting,
Crau's mortal passadge : too looke toe the sky she repyneth.
And toe put her purpose forward, this light toe relinquish,
When she the gift sacrifice with the incense burned on
  altars
(Grislye to bee spoaken) thee moysture swartlye was altred :
And the wyne, in powring, lyke blood black sootish apeered.
This too no creature, no, not to her sister is opned.
Further eke in the palaice a chapel fayre marbil abydeth,
Vowd to her first husband, which cel shee woorshiped
  highlye.
With whit lillye fleses, with garland greenish adorned :
Heere to her ful seeming she dyd hyre thee clamor of elfish
Goast of her old husband, her furth to this coompanye
  wafting,
When the earth with thee shaads of night was darcklye
  bemuffled.
Also on thee turrets the skrich howle, lyke fetchliefe ysetled,
Her burial roundel dooth ruck, and cruncketh in howling.
Sundrye such od prophecyes, many such prognosticat omens,
In foretyme coyned, theire threatnings terrible vtterd.
Yea cruel Æneas in dreame to her seemeth apeering,
Her furious chasing : her self left also, she deemed,
Post aloan, and soaly from woonted coompanye singled,
Too trauayl a iourney toe toe long, and that she returneth,
Too seek her owne Tyrians, through cragged passages
  vncooth.
Much lyke when Pentheus thee troups fel of hellish asemblye,
And two soons shyning, and two Thebs vaynely beholdeth.
Or lyke as, in skaffold theaters, is touzed Orestes
From his dame gastlye fleeing, with flam's and poysoned
  adders :
Or black scaalde serpents, and when that in entrye be setled

Sour feends grimlye gnashing, ramping with grislye reuengment.

When she thus in raging dyd swel : when plunged in anguish,
For to dye shee mynded, the mean and thee season apoincted,
Theese forged speeches to her sister sorroful vttring,
Shee shrowds her purpose, false hoape with phisnomye feigning.

   Sister, an od by knack haue I found (now rest ye triumphaunt)
Either this gadling shal swiftlye to mee be returned,
Or fro this hoat looue fits I shal bee shortlye retrayted.
Where the sun is woonted too set, neare the Ocean eending,
Thee last poinct farthest of dwellers Æthiop : Atlas
Mighty in this region bolsters thee starred Olympus.
From thence came a mayd priest, in soyle Massyla begotten,
Seixteen of Hesperides Sinagog, this sorceres vsed,
For too cram the dragon : she, on trees, slips consecrat heeded.
Hoonnye liquid sprinckling and breede sleepe wild popye strawing.
For to fre mynds, snared with looue, this Margerye voucheth,
Whom she wil, and oothers with loouetraps stronglye to fetter.
Also to stay the riuers, and back globs starrye returning.
In night too cooniure spirits : theare shal ye se (sister)
Thee ground right vnder too groane, trees bigge to fal headlong.
Thee Gods too witnesse, so thee, deare sister, I lykewise
Cal, bye thye sweet pallet, me this hard extremitye forceth
For to put in practise magical feats, sorcerye charming.
Wherefor in al secret let logs of tymber, in inner
Court, with speede, be reked, the sky with loftines hitting.
Also se, that thither you bring thee martial armoure,
That the peasaunt left heere, with al his misfortuned ensigns.
Theare bed must be placed, thee wedlock bed, where I, poore wretch,
Al my bane haue purchaste : theese rit's thee Cooniures asketh,
Too burne al monuments of this cursd villenus hoap loast.

This sayd, streight a silence shee keep's, her phisnomye
  paleth.
And yet An had nothing deemed, that Dido, the sister,
Preparde theese burials to her self, she no such furye casteth.
Or that woorse mischief might bee to her sister aproching,
Than when shee mourned the death of spouse soarye,
  Sichæus.
Thearefor her encheason shee purueys.
But the Queene, as tymber was broght, and piled in order,
And holme logs cleaued with cressets mounted ar added :
With twisted garland and leau's, spred greenlye, she garnisht
Thee place of her burial : there his armours al she reposed.
On the bed his picture shee set, ful playnely bethincking,
What would bee the sequel. There about stand consecrat
  altars :
With which eke embayed, the she priest, vntressed in heare
  locks,
Hundreds of the Godheds thrise tolde al giddylye calleth :
Shee crieth on the Erebus darcknesse and on Chaös hoch
  poch.
And the tripil dam Hecatee, with three faced angrye Diäna.
Shee pours eeke the liquours vntruely of founten Auernus.
Also by thee moone shyne yoong buds, scant spirted a booue
  ground,
Are soght too be loped with a brassye sieth : also the poyson
Cole black commixed with mylck : enquyrye was eke made,
For to snip, in the foaling, from front of fillye the knapknob
That the mare al greedy dooth snap.
Her self with presents standing neere the halloed altars,
Naked in her oane foote, with frock vnlaced aparralyd ;
Calleth at her parting on Gods : and destenye wytting
Thee stars : too the Godhead, with meeke submission, hartlye
Shee prayeth : yf deitee with no loare rightlye regadeth
Thee slip of al faythlesse break leages, that vnequalye looued.
  Neere toe dead of midnight yt drew, when member of
    eeche thing

Quick, and fore labored was, with sweet slumber, atached.
Thee woods are noyselesse, thee seas late stormye be calmed.
Thee stars from the sky top with glyding slipprye be shooting:
Thee fields and the catal bee mum: most queintlye bedecked
Fayre fowls, close lurcking in lak's, or shrowded in hard bed
Of thorny thickets, through rural countrye be napping,
In the silent nyghtyme, from thogt theire daytoyl amoouing.
But the poore vnresting Dido could catch no such happye
Season, too be quiet, shee sleeples is onlye remayning.
Now routs of carcking troubles, with sighs, be resorting:
Soomtyme fits tickling of her old looue in hertroote ar itching.
Then fresh on a suddeyn shee frets, and warpeth in anger.
And bayted in tugging skirmish then thus she bethoght her.
  What shal I doo therefore? shal I now, lyke a castaway
    milckmadge,
On myewoers formoure bee fawning? Too Nemod emprour
Now shal I meeke be suing, oft by mee coylye refused?
Therefor I must swiftly too Troian nauye be trudging,
Theare me toe bynd prentise, theyr wil, lyk a gally slaue,
    heeding.
And reason I trauayled too theym, that, by me so shielded,
My formoure beneficts defrayde so kindelye requited.
Wel, wel: graunt I trauayld, who would mee suffer? or of
    theym
What man, in his vessel, prowd borne, would carrye me
    scorned?
And alas, ô selly woomman: yeet must ye be lessond
Thee freaks, thee fickle promise, thee periurye Troian?
What then? with my fleeing shal I track theire nauye
    triumphing?
Or shal I pursu theym with strong and furnished armye?
And my pepil subiect, that I broght from Sidon in hazard
Of liefe, too the sea ward with danger shal they be pressed?
Nay, nay, thye self slaughter: thy bad lief vnhappye death
    asketh.
Thow, thow, deere sister, with my tears woommanish anguisht,

With my phrensie moued, to my foa dydst cast me ful open.
Might not I my lief tyme, lust fleshly and sinful auoyding,
Spend lyk an vnreasoned wild beaste, and such care abandon ?
I kept no promise to the boans of godlye Sichæus.
    Such playnts and quarrels in burnt brest stronglye she
      crusshed.
Now the good Æneas embarckt in vessel of hudgnesse,
Certen of his passadge, dyd sleepe : things duelye wel
    orderd.
Then toe the same captayne valiant, in slumber, apeered
Thee selfe same visadge, that face, that phisnomye bearing
In color, in speaking, thee self same Mercurye likning,
Forseene in his goulden fine locks, and youthlye resem-
    blaunce.
Thus thee wight sleeping with a newcoom message he greeteth.
    Thow sun of heunlye Godesse, dar'st thow to slumber in
      hazards ?
See ye not, ô madman, what dangers sundrye betyde you ?
Heyre ye not, in listning, thee westerne fortunat huffling ?
Shee coyn's cursd dangers, and mischiefs forgeth on anuyl.
Too dye she stands resolut : shee stormeth sweltred in anger.
Wil ye not haste swiftly, whilst leasur is offred of hastning ?
Perdye ye shal shortly perceaue, thee seas toe be coouerd,
With boats, and flaming fyre worcks toe be flasshed of eeche
    syde
Thee shoars, yf dawning in this fel countrye shal hold you.
On loa, cut of loytring, a wind fane changabil huf puffe
Always is a woomman. Thus sayd, through nightfog he
    vannisht.
    Then the duke Æneas, with shaddow sudden agrysed,
Vp starts from slugish sleeping, and coompanye waketh.
My men arise swiftly : to the tacklings speedelye stick yee :
Hoise sayl's with posting : for a God from celical heunseats
Sent, toe fle commaunds vs : lykewise toe cut hastlye the
    cabels.
Loa yet agayne spurs hee. We rely toe thyn hautye behestings

Who th'wart, mightye Godhead ; thus agayne toe thy wil we
    be forward.
Send thye pliaunt seruaunts thye good ayde, let stars of
    Olympus
Lucky assist the viadge: thus he sayd : then naked his edgd
    sword
Brandisht from the scabard hee drew: thee cabil he swappeth.
Al they the lyke poste haste dyd make, with scarboro
    scrabbling.
From the shoare owt sayle they: thee sea with great fleet is
    hooueld.
Fluds they rake vp spuming, with keele froth fomye they
    furrow.
    Thee next day foloing lustring Aurora lay shymring,
Her saffrond mattresse leauing to her bedfelo Tithon.
Thee Queene, when the daylight his shining brightnes
    afurded,
Peeps from loftye beacons, and sayling nauye beholdeth.
Thee stronds and the hauens of vessels emptye she marcketh.
Thrise, nay she foure seasons on fayre brest mightely
    bouncing,
And her heare owt rowting yellow: God Iuppiter, ogh lord:
Quod she, shal hee scape thus ? shal a stranger geue me the
    slampam ?
With such departure my regal segnorye frumping?
Shal not al oure subiects pursu with clamorus hu crye?
With my fleete hoate foloing shal not theire nauye be burned?
On men; alarme; fyrebrands se ye take; sails hoyse; roa
    ye swiftly:
What chat I foole? What place me doth hold? What
    phrensye me witcheth?
ô forlorne Dido, now now wrawd destenye grubs the.
This spite should be plyed, when thow thy auctoritye
    yeeldedst.
Marck the fayth and kindnesse, that he shews, who is soothlye
    reported,

Too carry his rellicques and countreye domestical house goods,
And to clap on shoulders his bedred graueporer old syre.
Could not I with my power both haue hackt and minced eke
    inchemeale
Thee coystrels carcasse, next in the sea deepelye toe drenche
    yt ?
Could not I then murther, with swoord, his coompanye
    stragling ?
Yea the lad Ascanius wel I might haue slaughtered, after
At tabil of the father too set thee chield to be maunged.
Thee chaunce in battayle, ye wil hold, is doubtful : I graunt yt.
What man had I feared, toe dye prest ? I had flamed of
    eechesyde
Theare tents and nauy, thee child, and thee father eending.
Yea the race extirping : my self had I walloed on theym.
ô sun in heune hye beaming, who behold'st ful woorckes al
    earthlye :
Of theese drirye dolours eeke thow Queene Iuno the
    searchresse,
And Godes hauty Hecatee, that dooest wights terrifye nightlye
In pathways traueling, ye bug hags fierce set to reuengments,
You Gods al mustring to the eende of wretched Elisa,
Eare this ; I doe craue you : for sin's due torture amoouing.
Lysten too my prayers. Yf this false traytor in hauen
Of force must be placed, toe the land yf destenye fling
    hym,
If faets of the Godheds so wil : theyre wyl be don hardly.
Yet let thee rascal with soldiours doughtye be lugged,
Spoyled of his weapons, wandring lyke a bannished owtlaw :
Haalde from the embracing of his onlye belooued Iülus :
And to beg his succoure : too see the funeral eendinges
Wretched of his kynred : lykewise when he shal be relying
Too streict condicions of peace, to vnlawful agreement :
In wisht Princelye quiet let not thee cullion harboure :
But before his fixed death tyme let his eende be cut hastlye,
In nauel of quicksands his corps vntumbed abyding.

Theese poincts humblye craue I, with blood this last wil I
stablish.
And you my Tyrian subiects, this linnage heere after
Pursue with hate bitter, this gift se ye graunt toe myne
ashes.
Let no looue or lyking, no fayth nor leage be betweene you,
Let there one od captayne from my boans rustye be
springing,
With fire eke and weapons thee caytiefs Troian auenging:
Now; then; at eeche season; what so eare streingth
mightye shal happen,
Let shoare bee too shoars, let seas contrarye toe seas stand,
And to armours, armours I do pray, let progenye bicker.
   Shee sayde; eke her vexte mynd shee tost and tumbled in
      ecche syde,
From thee light vnsauerye to flit, with gredines, asking.
Shee speaks too Barsen thee nurse of seallye Sichæus
(For then her owne mylckdame in byrth soyl was breathles
      abyding)
   Good nurse take the trauayle, too bring my sister An
      hither.
With the waters streaming let her hoale corps hastlye be
clensed.
Thee beasts bring she with her, with theym thee forenoted
offrings.
Thus let her haste hither: let thy pate godlye be coouerd.
Too the God infernal what rits bye me bee readye, furth
with
For to ende I purpose, my troubles wholye to finnish:
And toe put in fyre brands this Troian pedlerye trush trash.
   This sayd: shee trots on snayling, lyk a tooth shaken old
      hagge.
But Dido affrighted, stift also in her obstinat onset,
Her bluddy eyes wheeling, her lyers with swart spot ydusked,
And eke al her visage waning with murder aproching,
Too the inner quadrant runneth, then madlye she scaleth

Thee top of her banefyers, his swoord shee grappleth in
    handling;
I say the swoord brandisht, toe such a wild part not
    apoincted.
When she the weeds Troian dyd marck, and sporte breder
    old bed:
In tears salt blubbring, in musing stiddye remayning,
Shee fel on her mattresse: theese woords for a farewel
    awarding.
    O my sweet old leauings, whilst mee good destenye suffred,
And God of his goodnesse you mee too pleasure alowed,
Take ye mye faynt spirit, mee from theese troubles abandon,
I liu'de and the trauayl, graunted by fortun, I traced:
Also my goast shortly too pits of lymboe shal hobble.
A citty I founded stately, thee wals dyd I see rasd.
And the death of my husband on freendlesse broother I venged.
Blessed had I rested, yee thrise most blessed, yf onlye
In theese my regions no Troian vessel had anchord.
    Thus she sayd, and thrusting in couche her phisnomye
    cheerelesse,
But shal I dy sheepe lyke, not taking kindlye reuengment?
Yea wil I dy, quod shee, what? so? yea, so wyl I pack
    hence.
Let the cruel Troian, this flame from mayne sea beholding,
His panch now satiat, with this my destenye fatal.
    Thus she sayd; and falling on blade with desperat offer,
Her damsels viewd her: thee swoord al bluddye begoared,
And hands owt spreading they beheeld; thee raisd crye doth
    eccho
In the palaice: Rumor thee death through cittye doth vtter.
With sighs, with yelling, with skrich, with woommanish
    howling,
Thee rafters rattle: with shouts thee perst skye reboundeth.
With no les hudge bawling, than yf al Carthago wer enterd
By the enymy riffling, with flaming flasshye toe scorch al
Thee roofs of tenements, of Gods the consecrat howses.

Furth runs her sister, theese newes vnfortunat hyring,
With nayles hir visadge skratching, and mightilye rapping
Her brest with thumping frap knocks, through rout she doth
    enter,
And the dying sister, with roaring, lowdlye she named.
    Was this, deere sister, youre drift? therefore ye begyld
    me?
And for theese bancquets made I fiers, and halloed altars?
What shal I first mourne now, poore caytief, desolat
    owtwayle?
In this youre parting youre sisters coompanye skornd you?
Had ye toe that blood shot mee byd : wee both, with one
    edgtoole,
And eke in one moment, oure passadge fatal had ended.
This labor endurd I toe this ende? waste therefor I called
On Gods, from thye dying sharp pangs to be, wretch cruel
    absent.
The and my self haue I quight forlorne, thee nation hautye
Of Sidon, thy woorthye pepil, thy towne braue I batterd.
Speedelye bring me water, thee greene wound swiftlye toe
    souple;
And yf in her carcasse soom wind yeet softlye be breathing,
With lip I wil nurse yt : thus sayd shee climd toe the
    woodpile,
Claspt in her arms bracing thee panting murtheres haulf-
    quick,
With grunt wyde gasping: thee blackned gellyeblud,
    hardning,
Shee skums with napkins; shee would haue lifted her eyebal,
Feeble agayne weixing shee droups; thee deadlye push yrcks
    her.
Thrise she dyd endeuoure, too mount and rest on her elbow;
Thrise to her bed sliding shee quayls, with whirlygig eyesight
Vp to the sky staring, with belling skrichcrye she roareth,
When she the desyred soonbeams with faynt eye receaued.
    Then Iuno omnipotent long pangs, with mercye beholding,

And this her hard passadge: dyd send, from propped
    Olympus.
Thee lustring raynebow, from corps the spirit auoyding,
With rustling coombat buckling, with slayne bodye iustling.
For where as her parture noe due death, nor destenye
    caused,
But before her season thee wretch through phrensye was
    ended,
Her locks gould yellow therefore Proserpina would not
Shaue from her whit pallet, ne her ding too damnable Orcus.
   Than loa the fayre Raynebow saffronlyke feathered,
    hoou'ring
With thowsand gay colours, by the soon contrarye reshyning,
From the skye downe flickring, on her head moste ioyfulye
    standing,
Thus sayd : I doo Gods heast, from corps thy spirit I sunder.
Streight, with al, her fayre locks with right hand speedelye
    snipped :
Foorth with her heat fading, her liefe too windpuf auoyded.

FINIS.

Deo Gratias.

Opus decem dierum.

Other Poetical Devices.

HEERE AFTER ENSVE

CERTEYN PSALMES OF

Dauid, translated in too *English*,

according to thee obseruation

of thee *Latin* verses.

S thee *Latinists* haue diuerse kindes of verses besydes the *Heroiacal* : so our *English* wyl easelye admyt theym, althogh in thee one language or oother they sowne not al so pleasinglie too the eare (by whose balance thee rowling of thee verse is too bee gaged) as the sole *heroical*, or the *heroical* and thee *elegiacal* enterlaced one with the oother.

I haue made proofe of the *Jambical* verse in thee translation of the first *Psalme* of *Dauid*, making bold with thee curteous readei, too acquaynt hym there with.

THEE FIRST PSALME OF DAVID,

named in Latin, *Beatus vir*, translated

in too English Iambical verse.

Hat wight is happy and gratious,
That tracks noe wicked coompanye ;
Nor stands in il mens segnorye :
In chayre ne sits of pestilence.

2 But in the sound law of the lord
   His mynd, or heast is resiaunt :
   And on the sayd law meditat's,
   With hourlye contemplation.

3 That man resembleth verelye
   The graffe bye riuer situat ;
   Yeelding abundant plentines
   Of fruict, in haruest seasoned.

4 With heunlye ioyce stil nurrished
   His leafe bye no means vannisheth ;
   What thing his hert endeuoureth,
   Is prosperously accomplished.

5 Not so the sinful creaturs,
   Not so there acts are prosperous ;
   But lyke the sand, or chaffye dust,
   That wynddye pufs fro ground doe **blow.**

6 Therefor in houre iudicial,
   The vngodlye shal vnhaunst **remayne;**
   And shal be from the coompanye
   Of holye men quite sundered.

7 Because the lord preciselye knows
   The godlye path of goastlye men ;
   The fleshlye trace of filthye deeds
   Shal then be cleene extinguished.

Oo my seeming (wheather I am caryed too that
conceit by the vnacquaynted nooueltye, or the
meigernesse of this kind of verse) the *Iämbical*
quantitye relisheth soom what vnsauorlye in oure

language, being in truth not al too geather of thee tooth-soomest in thee *Latin*.

Thee *Hexametre* entermingled with the *Pentametre* doothe carrye a good grace in the *English*, as also among thee *Latins* : in which kind I haue endeuoured thee translation of thee secund *Psalme*.

THEE SECVND PSALME *QVARE*
fremuerunt gentes, translated in too
English Heroical and Elegiacal verse.

1 Yth franticque madnesse why frets thee multitud heathen ?
   And to vayn attemptings what furye sturs the pepil?

2 Al thee worldlye Regents, in clustred coompanye, crowded,
   For toe tread and trample Christ with his holye godhead.

3 Breake we there hard fetters, wee that be in Christian houshold,
   Also from oure persons pluck we there yrnye yokes.

4 Hee skorns theire woorcking, that dwels in blessed Olympus :
   And at thiere brainsick trumperye follye flireth.

5 Then shal he speake too those in his hard implacabil anger,
   And shal turmoyle theym, then, with his heauye furye.

6 I raigne and doe gouerne, as king, by the lord his apoinctment,
   Of mount holye Siωn ; his wyl eke heunlye preaching.

7 Thee father hath spoaken : thow art my deerelye begotten ;
   This day thy person for my great issue breding.

8 Too mee frame thye prayers, eke of ethnicks the heyre wil
    I make the,
      Also toe thy seisin wyde places earthlye giue I.

9 With the rod hard steeled thow shalt theyre villenye
    trample ;
      Lyke potters pypkin naghtye men easlye breaking.

10 You that ar earthlye Regents, Iudges terrestrial harcken,
      With the loare of vertu warelye too be scholed.

11 Too God youre seruice with fearful duitye betake yee ;
      With trembling gladnesse yeeld to that highnes honor.

12 Lerne wel youre lessons, least that God ruffle in anger,
      And fro the right stragling, with furye snacht, ye perish.

13 When with swift posting his dangerus anger aprocheth,
      They shal bee blessed which in his help be placed.

IN thee secund verse I translate, *Christe with his
heunlye Godhead, and yeet thee *Latin* renneth, *aduersus
dominum et aduersus Christum eius.* Wherein I offer no
violence too thee mynd and meaning of thee *Prophet.* For his
drift in this *Psalme* tendeth too thee reclayming of earthlye
potentats from thee vayne enterprice they take in hand, in thee
suppressing of *Christ* his kingdoom : which by two meanes hathe
beene attempted. Thee one when oure *Saluioure* was heere in
thee earthe, whom thee *Iewes* and *gentils* crucified : thee oother
after his *Ascention*, when his *elect* weare and now are daylye
persecuted by thee *miscreaunts*, which persecution *Christ*
Act. 9. 4.   dooth accoumpt his *owne*, as when he challenged
Saul, hee demaunded why he dyd persecute hym : accoumpting thee *persecution* of his *members* too be his *owne.* And to
thee lyke purpose thee *apostels* applye this *Psalme* in thee 4. of
Actor. 4. 25.   the *Actes.* Now thee *Prophet* vnfoldeth thee vanitye
of thee *Iewes* and *gentils* in conspiring too geather too
surprice thee regiment of *Christe*, in that hee is *God*, and
that he is the *eternal Soon* of thee *father*, too whom al *power*

is geeuen in *heuen* and *earth*, as wel with iustice Matt. 23. 18.
too crushe thee reprobat, as with mercye too salue thee elect.
Therefor yt standeth with thee meaning of thee *Prophet*, too
aduouch thee empugning of *Christ*, too bee the impugning of
God, in that hee is both *God* and *man : God* of thee Athan in
substance of his *father* begotten before thee worlds, Symb.
and *man* of thee substance of his *moother* borne in thee
world. And that thee *soon* was before al worlds begotten of
thee *father* is playnelye notified in thee seuenth verse, where
thee *jather* sayeth too thee *soon*, this *day I haue begotten thee* :
signifiing, by *this day*, *Eternitye* : in which generation is
neither tyme to coom, nor tyme past, nor anye changeable
season, but alwayes thee self same immutable *eternitye* too
bee considered. And therefor in thee 12. verse, thee *Prophet*
layeth downe an exhortation too theese men of state, not
onlye not too band agaynst *Christe*, but also too submit
theymselues too his loare, as too *God*, who would haue his
soon honored : which verse I haue translated according too
thee vulgar edition, *apprehendite disciplinam*, where with thee
Greek text δράξασθε παιδίας, and also the *Chaldye* interpretoure
agreeth, as *Petrus Galatinus* hath obserued : yeet Petrus Galat.
the *Hebrue Nas ku bar*, or *Nassecu Bar*, may bee too de archan.
Catho. Veri.
more aduantadge of vs *Christians*, and too thee con- lib. 3. cap. 6.
fusion of thee *Iewes* ootherwise translated. *S. Hierom* turneth
yt, *adore purely*, or *adore thee soon*, which approoueth Hierony. in
thee deitye of *Christ* : *Felix* translateth yt, *kisse thee* Psal. 2.
soon, or *embrace the soon :* wherein also the prerogatiue of
Christ is manifested. For by thee *kissing of thee soon* is
signifyed thee embracing of his power and doctrin : which
hath beene deliuered from thee mouth of thee *almightye* too
his seruauntes by thee handes of his *Prophets* and *Apostles*.
And therefore thee auncient *Talmudistes* expound, in this
wise, that of thee *Canticles, Osculetur me osculo oris* Canti. 1. 1.
sui, let hym kisse mee with thee kisse of his owne mouth :
that is, let thee *Messias*, who is the soon of *God*, instruct mee
with his owne mouth. Let not *Moyses* bee sent, who is

Exod. 4. 10.
Eſai. 6. 5.
Ierem. 1. 6.

tongue tyed : nor *Esaias*, that acknowlegeth his lips too bee polluted ; Nor *Ieremye*, that sayd hee could not speake ; but let thee verye *soon* of God, who is thee *fathers* wisdoom and force coom, and with his mouth lesson and instruct mee. So that al beyt thee word (*Bar*) may emport soomtyme learnyng, soomtyme corne, soomtyme that which is pure or cleene, yet eftsoons yt notifieth a sunne. As *Barptolomeus*, yf we respect the *etymologye* of thee woord,

Hieron. in
apologi. cont.
Ruffin. cap. 5

signifieth thee *soon* of *Ptolomeus*, *Barnabas*, thee *soon* of a *Prophet*, as is learnedly expounded by *S. Hierom* in his *apologye* agaynst *Ruffinus*.

 ut too returne too oure *English* verses, I haue attempted thee translation of thee third *Psalme* in thee *Asclepiad* kind : which also, in my phantasye, is not also pleasaunt in thee *English* : but that I refer too thee iudgment of thee reader.

THEE THIRD PSALME, NAMED,
Domine, quid multiplicati sunt, translated in too English Asclepiad verse.

1　Ord, my drirye foes why doe (they) multiplye ?
　　Mee for too ruinat sundrye be coouetous.
　　　2 Hym shields not the godhead, sundrye say too mye soule.

3　Th'art, lord most vigilant, wholye my succorer,
　　And in the al mye staying shal be stil harbored :
　　Tw'art my most valiant victorye glorious.

4　To our lord lowd I cryed : from holye place herd he mee.

5   In graue new buryed fast haue I slumbered.
    I rose too liefe agayn through God his hollines.

6   I feare not furious multitud infinit,
    With coompasse laboring, my body for toe catche.
    Rise Lord omnipotent, help me, mye champion.

7   Lord, thy cleere radiaunt righteus equitye
    Hath squisd al mye foes, falslye me ransaking.

8   Oure Lord participats saulftye with happines :
    With gifts, heunlye Godhead, thy pepil amplye blisse.

Vt of al theese bace and foot verses (so I terme al sauluing thee *Heroical* and *Elegiacal*) thee *Saphick*, too my seeming, hath thee prehemynencye, which kind I haue assayed in thee paraphrastical translation of thee fourth *Psalme*.

THEE FOVRTH PSALME, NAMED,
Cùm inuocarem, paraphrasticalye translated in too English Saphick verse.

1   Hen that I called, with an humbil owtcrye,
    Thee God of Iustice, meriting mye saulftye,
    In many dangers mye weake hert vpholding
       Swiftlye dyd hyre mee.

2   Therefor al freshly, lyke one oft enured
With thye great goodnesse, yet agayne doe craue thee,
Mercye too render, with al eeke toe graunt mee
       Gratius harckning.

3   Wherefore of mankind ye that are begotten,
      What space and season doe ye catche for hardnesse,
      Vanitee loouing, toe toe fondlye searching
                Trumperye falshood.

4   Know ye for certeyn, that our heunlye rectoure
      His sacred darling specialye choosed :
      And the lord therefor, when I pray, wil harcken
                Too mye requesting.

5   For syn expyred se ye rest in anger,
      And future trespas, with al haste, abandon :
      When that in secret ye be fleashlye tickled,
                Run toe repentaunce.

6   Righteous incense sacrifice heere after
      In God, oure guider, your hole hoape reposing.
      Fondlye doo diuerse say, what hautye great lord
                Vs doth inhable.

7   Thy star of goodnesse in vs is reshining,
      Sound reason graunting, with al heunlye coomfort :
      With these hudge presents toe myne hert afurding
                Gladnes abundant.

8   Theare wheat and vineyards, that ar haplye sprouting,
      And oyle, in plenty toe the store cel hurded,
      With pryde, and glorye to the stars inhaunceth
                Worldlye men huffing.

9   Thogh that I see not, with a carnal eysight,
      Thee blis and glory, that in heun is harbourd :
      Yeet with hoape stand I, toe be theare reposed,
                And toe be resting.

10   By reason that thow, my God heunlye, setledst
     Mee, thye poore seruaunt, in hoape, and that highlye :
     Too be partaker with al heunlye dwellers
          Of thye blis happye.

A PRAYER TOO THEE TRINITYE.

Rinitee blessed, deitee coëqual,
     Vnitee sacred, God one eeke in essence,
     Yeeld toe thy seruaunt, pitifullye calling
          Merciful hyring.
Vertuus liuing dyd I long relinquish,
Thy wyl and precepts miserablye scorning,
Graunt toe mee, sinful pacient, repenting,
          Helthful amendment.
Blessed I iudge hym, that in hert is healed :
Cursed I know hym, that in helth is harmed :
Thy physick therefore, toe me, wretch vnhappye
          Send, mye Redeemer.
Glorye too God, thee father, and his onlye
Soon, the protectoure of vs earthlye sinners,
Thee sacred spirit, laborers refreshing,
          Stil be renowmed.   Amen.

HEERE AFTER ENSVE
CERTAYNE POËTICAL
CONCEITES.

A diuise made by *Virgil*, or rather by soom oother vpon a Riuer so hard frozen, that waynes dyd passe ouer yt : varyed sundrye wayes, for commendacion, as yt should seeme, of the *Latin* tongue, and thee same varietye dubled in thee *English*.

1 *Va ratis egit iter, iuncto boue, plaustra trahuntur;*
Postquam tristis hyems frigore vinxit aquas.

2 *Sustinet vnda rotam, patulæ modò peruia puppi :*
Vt concreta gelu marmoris instar habet.

3 *Quas modò plaustra premunt vndas, ratis antè secabat :*
Postquam brumali diriguere gelu.

4 *Vnda rotam patitur, celerem nunc passa carinam :*
In glaciem solidam versus vt amnis abit.

5 *Quæ solita est ferre vnda rates, fit peruia plaustris :*
Vt stetit in glaciem marmore versa nouo.

6 *Semita fit plaustro, quà puppis adunca cucurrit :*
Postquam frigoribus bruma coëgit aquas.

7 *Orbita signat iter, modò quà cauus alueus exit :*
Strinxit aquas tenues vt glacialis hyems.

8 *Amnis iter plaustro dat, qui dedit antè carinæ :*
Duruit vt ventis vnda, fit apta rotis.

9 *Plaustra boues ducunt, quà remis acta carina est :*
Postquam diriguit crassus in amne liquor.

10 *Vnda capax ratium plaustris iter algida præbet :*
Frigoribus sæuis vt stetit amnis iners.

11 *Plaustra viam carpunt, quà puppes ire solebant :*
Frigidus vt Boreas obstupefecit aquas.

THEE SAME ENGLISHED.

1 Heare ships sayld, the wagons are now drawn
    stronglye with oxen :
    For that thee season frostye dyd hold the water.
2 Theare the wagon runneth, wheare whillon vessel hath
    hulled :
    For that thee marbil frostye made hard the riuer.
3 Theare placed is the wagon, wheare boats road grapled at
    anchour :
    When that a could wynter thee water hastye stayed.
4 Now the car is trayled, wheare barges latelye repayred :
    When that cold Boreas chillye did hold the riuer.
5 Where ships haue trauayled, theare now cars sundrye be
    tracing :
    When nipping wynter thee riuer hardlye stoped.
6 Theare the coch is running, wheare latelye the nauye
    remayned :
    When that the northen frostye gale hemd the riuer.
7 Now the naue hath passage, wheare the keele was latelye
    reposed :
    By reason of wynters frost, that hath hyd the water.
8 Thee water vp the wagons dooth prop, that vessel hath
    harbourd :
    Beecause that the riuer frostines ysye tyed.
9 Now the wagon rowleth, wheare lighturs hulled in hauen :
    When that a frost knitting stronglye witheeld the riuer.
10 Wheare the ship earst sayled, the cart his passage on
    holdeth :
    When thee frostye weather thee water hardlye glued.
11 Now the wayn is propped, whear to earst thee gallye
    resorted :
    For that thee winters hoare glue reteynd the water.

SO MANY TYMES IS THE *LATIN*

varyed, and yeet as manye tymes more. for the
honoure of thee English.

1   Heare chariots doe trauayle, wheare late the great
argosye sayled :
By reason of the riuer knit with a frostye soder.

2 Wheare the great hulck floated, theare now thee cartwheele is hagling :
Thee water hard curded with the chil ysye rinet.

3 Where skut's furth launched, theare now the great wayn
is entred :
When the riuer frized by reason of the weather.

4 Wheare rowed earst mariners, theare nowe godye carman
abydeth,
Thee flud, congealed stiflye, relats the reason.

5 Now the place of sayling is turnd to a carter his entrye,
This change thee winters chillines hoarye bredeth.

6 Now wayns and chariots are drawne, wheare nauye dyd
harrow :
This new found passadge frostines hoarye shaped.

7 Wheare barcks haue passed, with cart's that parcel is
haunted :
From woonted moysture for that ice heeld the water.

8 Wheare stems haue trauersd, there haue oxen traced in
headstal :
By reason yse knitting thee water heeld froe floing.

9 Wheare the flye boat coasted, theare cart wheels clustred
ar hobling
This new strange passadge winter his hoarnes habled.

10 Earst the flud, vpbearing thee ship, now the cartwheele
vpholdeth.
When water is ioygned firmlye with hoarye weather.

11 Whear ruther steered, thee goad theare poaked hath
oxen :
Thee winters coldnesse thee riuer hardlye roching.

Thee description of *Liparen*, expressed by *Virgil* in
thee eight booke of his *Æneis*, in which place, thee
Poët played, as yt weare, his price, by aduauncing
at ful thee loftines of his veyne: doon in too
English by thee translatoure for his last farewel
too thee sayd *Virgil*.

W'ard *Sicil* is seated, toe the welken loftelye peaking,
A soyl, ycleapt *Liparen*, from whence, with flownce
furye slinging,
Stoans, and burlye bulets, lyke tamponds, maynelye be
towring.
Vnder is a kennel, wheare Chymneys fyrye be scorching
Of *Cyclopan* tosters, with rent rocks chamferye sharded,
Lowd dub a dub tabering with frapping rip rap of *Ætna*.
Theare stroaks stronglye threshing, yawl furth groans,
stamped on anuyl.
In the den are drumming gads of steele, parchfulye sparck-
ling;
And flam's fierclye glowing from fornace flasshye be whisking.
Vulcan his hoate fordgharth, namde eeke thee *Vulcian* Island.
Downe from the heunlye palace trauayled thee fyrye *God*
hither.
In this caue the rakehels yrne bars, bigge bulcked, ar
hamring.
Brotes, and *Steropes*, with baerlym swartye *Pyracmon*.
Theese thre were vpbotching, not shapte, but partlye wel
onward,
A clapping fyerbolt (such as oft, with rownce robel hobble,
Ioue toe the ground clattreth) but yeet not finnished holye.
Three *showrs* wringlye wrythen glimring, and forceblye
sowcing;
Three watrye *clowds* shymring toe the craft they rampyred
hizing,
Three *wheru's* fyerd glystring, with *Soutwynds* rufflered
huffling.

Now doe they rayse gastly lyghtnings, now grislye rebound-
    ings
Of ruffe raffe roaring, mens herts with terror agrysing.
With peale meale ramping, with thwick thwack sturdelye
    thundring.
Theyre labor hoat they folow: toe the flame fits gyreful
    awarding.
And in an od corner, for *Mars* they be sternfulye flayling
Hudge spoaks and chariots, by the which thee surlye *God*,
    angerd,
Hastye men enrageth, too wrath towns bat'ful on eggeth.
And they be fresh forging toe the netled *Pallas* an armoure,
With gould ritchlye shrined, wheare scaals be ful horriblye
    clincked
Of scrawling *serpents*, with sculcks of poysoned *adders*.
In brest of the Godesse *Gorgon* was cocketed hardlye,
With nodil vnioyncted, by death, light vital amoouing.
Voyd ye fro these flamfews, quoa the *God*, set a part the
    begun wurck.

THEE LOOVER LONG SOGHT VN-

too by his freend, at last repayreth too her presence :
and after a fevv meetinges smelling thee drift of thee
moother, vvhich earst hee dyd forcast, too tend too
the preferring of her daughter in marriadge, refray-
neth the gentlevvomans coompanye, thogh eftsoones
too thee contrarye sollicited, as one vnwylling too
marry at al, and verye loath too mar so curteous a
dame : and therfor, for thee preseruation of her
honoure, and too auoyd the encoumbrance of *looue*,
hee curbeth *affection* vvith *discretion*, and thus
descanteth on the playne song.

Ntoe this hard passadge (good God) what phrensye
    dyd hale mee ?
From thye quiet seruice my self too slau'rye betaking.

Vntoe the lure smoothly, with faynd solemnitye, trayned.
Fiue moonths ful she plyed: means made: dreams sundrye
related.
If we met in walcking, what scarlet blush she resembled?
Her color oft altreth: with loou's hoat palsye she trembleth.
Back goth her eye glauncing: a sigh herd; moods chaung-
abil vttred.
I litle accoumpted, God knows, thee curtesye proferd.
Stil dyd I keepe backward, what I find, tym's sundrye
forvttring.
For toe loue a stranger, scarce seene, what sound reason egs
her?
But reason in loouepangs who seeketh? a wooman eke hateth,
Or loou's extreemely: no meane, no measure is extant.
At length woon bye prayer to her lodge my passage I bended;
Lumps of looue promist, nothing perfourmed in earnest.
Forgerye thee pandar: thee messadge mockrye: the moother
Thee knot of al the lying, thee virgin faultles is onlye.
But shal I looue the lady, so as Petrarck Laura regarded?
In paper her dandling? her person neauer atayning?
Such sport fits the Poëts, whom rauing phantasye sotteth.
I doe wake, I dreame not: noe such ynckhorne vanitye feeds
mee.
Thee bodye, not shaddow: no woords, but wurckes I coouet.
Marriage is profred: that yoke thee loouer abhorreth.
And toe mar a virgin, to a freend such curtesye tendring,
Were not a practise honest, nor a preede toe be greatlye
recounted.
Thee *rinet* of freendship, *vertu*, such treacherye damneth.
What man of ennye reason with villenye vertue requyteth.
Rest the quiet therefore: flee from theese dangerus hard
rocks,
Whereto loue oft leadeth, with stormes thee passage is
haunted.
Great trauayl in the sueing, thee profred curtesye skorned.
If she coye, that kendleth thee fondling loouer his onset:

Greedelye wee coouet, that was to vs flatlye refused.
Queynt of a kisse publicque, lewd lust with nicitye masking.
Such woomens negatiues for a yeelding, *yea Syr*, ar holden.
What doth auayl, minion, this sleight and treacherye cogging.
Cleaue toe the sound *Castè*, flee from thee patcherye *Cautè*.
  Then fresh agayne prayeth hee, percase thee suitur is eared.
Wel: the woer gayneth the requyred victorye. What then?
Is the trauayl finnisht? are pleasurs onlye then hoouering?
Nay: then thy misery, thine hel eeke theare taketh his entraunce.
Now thye sleepe is scanted, now stinging iclosye fretteth.
Dame Venus and kingdooms can no riualitye suffer.
Her fauor hee gayned with a beck: that burneth in entrayls.
Who deems yt wisdoom with glasse too rampyre a Bulwarck?
Men say, that a changing of pasture maketh a fat calfe.
A Calf yt maketh; toe the fat let a grasier aunswere.
That wil a way, who can hold? such challeng therefor abandon.
Robbrye toe bee *purchase*, soom terme eeke *leacherye solace*.
  She kept no promise: that would be a quarrel in earnest.
Now wars proclaymed, peace agayne now freshlye renewed.
Now these suspicions, now that surmises ar opned.
Now beldam Brokresse must bee with moonnye rewarded.
Veritye detecting, noght els but vanitye babling.
This gowne your looue mate, that kyrtil costlye she craueth,
This pearle, that diamond, this massiue garganet asking.
Noght may ye forsake her: that would bee felonye deemed.
Iclosye thee person, thee purse eeke *penurye* pincheth.
Is this an heun, trow you? fro that heun Gods mercye wythold mee.
Pleasure is vnpleasaant that purchaseth heauye repentaunce.
In so much as therefore this great vexation haunteth
Al such as are loouers, and wished bootye doe coompasse:
I doe renounce flatly thee fielde, such victorye skorning,
Too mye fredoom formere my self from slauerye reclayming.

AN ENDEVOVRED DESCRIP-
tion of his *Mystresse*.

Ature in her woorcking soomtyme dooth pinche lyke a niggard,
Disfiguring creatures, lyms with deformitye dusking.
This man is vnioyncted, that swad lyke a monster abydeth ;
Shee limps in the going, this slut with a cammoysed haucks nose,
And as a Cow wasted plods on, with an head lyke a lutecase.
Theese faultes fond Hodipecks impute too Nature, as yf she
Too frame were not habil gems with rare dignitye lustring.
Wherefor in aduis'ment laboring too cancel al old blots,
And toe make a patterne of price, thee maystrye toe pubblish:
For toe shape a peerlesse paragon shee mynded, asembling
Her force and cunning : for a spirt lands sundrye refusing,
And with al her woorckmat's trauayling shee lighteth in *Holland*,
Round too the *Hage* posting, to the world *Marye* matchles auauncing.
In bodye fine fewterd, a braue Brownnetta ; wel handled ;
Her stature is coomly ; not an ynch toe superfluus holding ;
Gratius in visadge ; with a quick eye prittelye glauncing ;
Her lips lyke corral rudye, with teeth lillye whit eeuened.
Yoong in age, in manners and nurture sage she remayneth ;
Bashful in her speaking, not rash, but watchful in aunswer ;
Her look's, her simpring, her woords with curtesye sweetning ;
Kynd and also modest ; lyking with chastitye lyncking ;
And in al her gesturs obseruing coomlye *Decorum*.
But toe what eend labor I, me toe presse with burden of Ætna :

Thee stars too number, poincts playnely vncounctabil opning.
Whust: not a woord: a silence such a task impossibil
    asketh.
Her *vertu* meriteth more prayse, than parlye can vtter.

HIS DEVISE WRYTTEN

in his *mystresses* booke.

*Aga Hollandorum vario splendore refulget;*
    Solis in hac lumen sola Maria *tenet.*

THEE SAME ENGLISHED.

Hee fine Hage excelleth with lusturs sundrye reshyn-
    ing,
    Thee Sun hath his brightnesse in *Marye* solye
    placed.

THREE ESPECIAL GIFTES,

wherein his *mystresse* excelleth.

Hree poincts my *mystresse* with passing dignitye
    garnish.
    Coomlynes of person thee first ranck rightlye reteig-
    neth:
Curtesye keeps the Secund: the third row *Chastitye* claymeth:
For so fayre a *Paragon*, with booxom deboynar vsadge;

And so pure a *Virgin*, with so rare vertue bedecked :
Sundrye may wel wish for. *Marye* must be the *Principal*
holden.

OF A CRAKING CVTTER,

extracted owt of Syr *Thomas Moore*
his Latin Epigrams.

Inckt was in wedlock a loftye Thrasonical huf snuffe :
In gate al on typstau's stalcking, in phisnomye daring.
This cutter valiant in warfare soght his auenture.
Thee whilst his minion, with carnal wantones itching,
Chooste for a freend secret no woorse, then a countrye lob
heerd swayne.
A pray for a paragon : but what ? thee knurrye knob oake tree,
Thogh craggy in griping, in strength surpasseth a smooth slip.
When Thraso from bickrings, not bluddye, returned is
homeward,
Of this hap aduertisde, with frantick iellosye taynted,
Hee seeks in thee fields, with swift enquirye, the riual.
Stay vagabund raskal (so he spake when he spyde the lob
heerd hyne)
Thee clowne stout standeth with a leshe of bulleted hard
stoans ;
Then Thraso with naked flatchet, with thunderus outcrye
Sayd : thow scuruye peasaunt, my wife th'hast, villen, abused.
My bed defiled : lyke a breaklooue mak'bat adultrer.
Al this I deny not, quoa the clowne : and what then : I pray
thee ?
Doost thow confesse yt ? Thraso sayd : bye the blessed
asemblye
Of the heunly sociats, hadst thow thy knauerye reneaged,
This mye blade in thye body should bee with speedines
hafted.

OF A TEMPEST QVAYLING

certeyn passengers borowed of thee same
Syr *Thomas Moore.*

Heare rose in sayling a rough tempestuus owtrage,
 With watryc plash bouncing, thee ribs of giddye ship
    hitting.
Thee mariners fearing, al hoap eeke of salftye reiecting,
Sayd: that a bad liuing eke a bad death rightlye requyred.
Al that are in passadge to a munck, father holye, resorted,
Who was eke embarcked, to hym theyre confession opning.
Howbeyt thee stormy ruffling is no whit abated;
But thee rough billows the ship toe toe terriblye charged.
Twish, what woonder is yt, quod one of thee coompanye,
    chauffing,
Yf that thee vessel with weight moste sinful is heauye.
Duck we the munck therefor, that al oure falts wholye
    receaued,
Hastlye let hym toe the seas oure syns and villenye carrye.
Al they be contented, thee munck they spedelye plunged:
Ceast was thee tempest, yf truth bee truelye related.
Heereby wee be scholed, what poyse sin ponderus holdeth,
That with an hudge and weightye balas surchargeth a vessel.

HESPERVS HIS CONFESSION,

written in Latin by the Sayd Syr *Thomas Moore.*

Esperus his faulty liuelood too cal toe recounting
 Mynding, too be shriuen with woont accustomed
    hastned.
When that he told playncly, what crym's most sinful he
    practisd,
Yeet thee goastlye father laboring more deepelye toe ransack
His formere liuing: by distinct article asked

Eu'rye sin, and naming by peecemeal curius eche fault,
At leingth demaunded, wheather, with sorcerye blinded,
Erst he beleefe yeelded toe the bugs infernal? here aunswerd
Hesperus: holye father, doe ye thinck me soe madly bewitched
Too beleue in the deuils? I tel you truelye, toe great payn's
Stil I take enduring, in God yeet scantlye beleeuing.

OF TYNDARVS, THAT FRVM-

ped a gentlewoman for hauing a long nose, deliuered
by the *former author* in Latin.

Yndarus attempting too kis a fayre lasse with a long
nose,
Would needs bee finish, with bitter frumperye
taunting.
In vayn I doo coouet my lips too linck toe thye sweete lips,
Thy nose, as a stickler, toe toe long vs parteth a sunder.
Heere the mayd al bashful, the vnsau'ry saucines heeding:
With choler oppressed, thus shrewdlye toe Tyndarus
aunswerd,
Syth mye nose owtpeaking, good syr, your liplabor hindreth,
Hardlye ye may kisse mee, where no such gnomon apeereth.

[From this point to the bottom of *p*. 147 (forming *pp*. 101–102 of the
original Leyden Edition), is wanting in the Ashburnham copy, and is
supplied only from that at Britwell.]

SYR THOMAS MOORE HIS

receipt for a strong breath translated
owt of his Latin Epigrames.

Irst for a strong sauoure stincking, a *leeke* may be taken:
That sent too bannish, thee best is an *Onion* eaten.
And toe repeal lykwise that sauoure, *garlik* is holsoom.
If that theese simples wyl not thee filthod abandon,
A *rose*, or els nothing that drafty infirmitye cureth.

HEERE AFTER ENSVE
CERTEYN EPITAPHES
framed as wel in *Latin*
as *English*.

AN EPITAPH DEVISED VPON

thee death of thee right honourable *James* earle of *Ormond* and *Ossorye*, who deceased at Elye house in Holborne about thee yeare 1546. thee xviij. of October. and lieth buryed in S. *Thomas Acres* church, Extracted owt of thee third booke of thee Historye of Ireland.

OR *patriæ fixum viuens, iam redditur illi
Post mortem, patriæ quæ peracerba venit.
Non sine corde valet mortalis viuere quisquam;
Vix tua gens vita permanet absque tua.
Quæ licet infælix extincto corde fruatur,
Attamen optato viuere corde nequit.
Ergo quid hæc faciat? quem re non possit amorem,
Cordi vt tam charo reddere corde velit.*

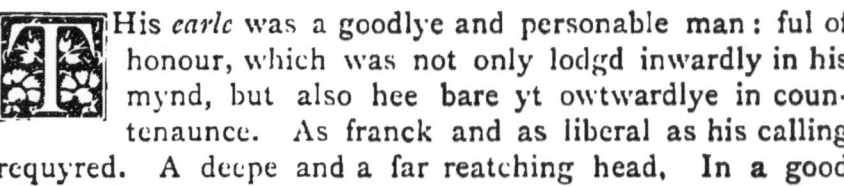

His *earle* was a goodlye and personable man : ful of honour, which was not only lodgd inwardly in his mynd, but also hee bare yt owtwardlye in countenaunce. As franck and as liberal as his calling requyred. A deepe and a far reatching head, In a good quarel rather stout then stubborne, bearing hym self with no less courage, when hee resisted, than with honourable discretion where hee yeelded. A fauourer of *peace*, no furtherer of *war*, as one that preferd vnlawfull quietnesse before vpright troubles, beeing notwyth standing of as great wisdom in thee

one, as of valour in thee other. An earnest and zealous vpholder
of his countrye, in al attemptes rather respecting thee publicque weale, than his priuat gayne. Wherebye hee bound his
countrye so greatly vntoo hym, that Ireland might with good
cause wish, that either hee had neauer beene borne, or elles
that hee had neauer deceased, so yt were lawful, too craue hym
immortal, that by course of nature was framed mortal. And
too giue sufficient proof of thee entyre affection hee bare his
countrye, and of thee zealouse care hee dyd cast thereon, hee
beetooke in his death bed his *soule* to *God*, his *carcasse* too
Christian burial, and his *hert* too his *countrye*, declaring thereby,
that where his mynd was setled in this liefe, his hert should
bee theare entumbed after his death. Which was according
too his wyl accomplisht. For his hert was conueighed in too
Ireland, and lyeth engraued in thee chore of thee cathedral
church in *Kilkennye*, where his aucetours, for thee more parte,
are buryed. Vpon which kind legacye thee abooue wrytten
Epitaph was deuised.

VPON THEE DEATH OF THEE

lord of thee owt Isles of *Scotland* : of whom
mention is made in thee third book
of thee Histor. of Ireland.

Ique manuque mea patriæ dum redditur exsul,
   Exsul in externa cogor et ipse mori.

His noble man assisting thee earle of *Lennox* eended
his lief at *Howth* presently vpon his arriual, and
was with great solemnitie buried in S. *Patrick*
his church at *Dublin* : circa Annum Domini
M. D. XLIII.

[From this point, the text continues to represent the collation of both
the Ashburnham and Britwell copies.]

VPON THEE DEATH OF HIS

father, *James Stanyhurst* Esquyer, who deceased at Dublyn Anno 1573. xxvij. of December, ætatis LI.

Ita breuis, mors sancta fuit (pater optime) visa :
Vita timenda malis, mors redamanda bonis.
Vrbs est orba sopho ; legum rectore tribunal ;
Causidicoque cliens ; atque parente puer.
Plurima proferrem, sed me prohibere videtur
Pingere vera dolor, fingere falsa pudor.
Non opus est falsis, sed quæ sunt vera loquenãa,
Non mea penna notet, buccina fama sonet.
Hoc scripsisse satis ; talem, quandoque, parentem
Est habuisse decus, sed caruisse dolor.
Filius hæc dubitans talem vix comperit vsquam
Vllus in orbe patrem, nullus in vrbe parem.
Mortuus ergo, pater, poteris bene viuus haberi,
Viuis enim mundo nomine, mente deo.

VPON THEE DEATH OF

his father in law *Syr Christofer Barnewal* knight.

Æta tibi, sed mæsta tuis mors accidit ista :
Regna dat alta tibi, damna dat ampla tuis.
Lætus est in cælis vllo sine fine triumphans,
Mæstus at in terris diues inopsque iacent.
Nam sapiente caret diues, qui parta gubernet,
Nec, qui det misero munera, pauper habet.
Te gener ipse caret, viduæ, te rustica turba,
Atque vrbana cohors te (Socer alme) caret

Non est digna viro talis respublica tanto,
 Nam sanctos sedes non nisi sancta decet.
Mira loquor, sed vera loquor, non ficta reuoluo,
 Si maiora loquar, nil nisi vera loquar.
Mortuus es? nobis hoc crimina nostra dederunt.
 Mortuus es? virtus hoc tibi sacra dedit.
Viuus es in cœlo, dedit hoc tibi gratia Christi,
 Viuus vt in mundo sis, tibi fama dabit.

Hristophorus Barnewallus, vir equestris ordinis, vetere ac illustri familia procreatus, cùm esset admodum adolescens ad clarissimam Oxoniensem Academiam à præstantissimis parentibus missus summè erat eloquentiæ atque philosophiæ studiosus. Quæ cùm magno studio curaque disceret; Londinum profectus est, vbi in hospitium Graiense cooptatus cognitionem Britannici iuris bene laudabilem erat consecutus. Cùm verò non multùm à tanti operis perfectione abesset, optimus et amantissimus eius pater hoc interim spacio (anima à corpore semota et disclusa) hinc demigrauit. Quo audito, Christophorus se statim in patriam, cum omnium applausu, contulit, atque ibi patrimonium suum, quod ei iam tum satis amplum pater reliquerat, summa æquabilitate ac recta conscientia, sine vllius offensione amplificauit. Mira erat vitæ eius integritas; prædicabilis erga deum sanctitas; admirabilis in patriam pietas. Nulla verò in tota regione erat hospitalitas, quæ vix posset cum illius hospitalitate conferri. Sapientia præditus profectò singulari. In vrbe gratia, ruri auctoritate florebat. Vir erat vt corpore, ita valetudine plærunque imbecillior, natura mitissimus, in iniurijs ferendis patientissimus, in repellendis fortissimus, in republicis defendenda acerrimus. Nono Calend. Augusti ex itinere in febrim incidit, cuius dolore paucis post diebus, cum totius reipublicæ, eiulatu ac lamentatione, consumtus est: annos natus 42. Anno Domini 1575.

VPON THEE DEATH OF HIS

wief *Genet*, daughter too Syr *Christofer Barnewal* knight, who deceased, at *Knight his bridge*, of Chieldbyrth, Anno 1579. August xxvj. ætatis xix. and lieth entered at *Chelsye*.

Ors tua quanta tuis mæroris vulnera fixit,
    Multorum gemitus, me reticente, sonant.
    Nobilis ortus erat, tua clarè vita peracta,
Corpore pulchra satis, moribus alma sacris.
Heu mihi, sed subitò sublata hæc dona fuerunt,
    In teneris annis dum mihi dona dabas.
Quam dederas natæ vitam, tibi nata negauit,
    Quam dederas lucem, luce (Genetta) cares.
Qualis erat mater (sola breuitate relicta
    Vitæ) sit talis nata relicta precor.
Quos iunxit mundo, Christus coniungat Olympo,
    Vt thorus vnus erat, sic thronus vnus erit.

VPON THEE DEATH OF THEE

right honourable and his moste deere coosen, thee *lord Baron of Louth*, who was trayterouslye murthred by *Mackmaughoun*, an Irish Lording, about thee yeere 1577.

Hus loa, thyne hast (coosen) bred waste too cittye,
    toe country.
Thee bearbrat boucher thy corps with villenye
    mangled.

Not by his manlye valour, but through thy desperat offer.
As the liefe is lasting too sutch, as in armes ar heedye,
Eun so death is posting too those, that in armor ar headye.
Haulfpenye, far better then an housful cluster of angels,
Althogh habil, would not fro thye danger deadlye be parted.
Whom lief combyned, death could not scatter a sunder.
Sutch is thee fastnesse of foster broothcrhod Irish.
Thogh Sydny and Deluyn thee murther partlye reuenged :
A losse so pretiouse may not bee fullye requited.
Thee death of a thowsand Maghouns is vnequal amendment.
Thee nobles may not but a death so bluddye remember,
Thee Plunckets wyl not from mynd such boutcherye bannish.
Thy Ladye, thy kinred doo misse thy freendship aprooued ;
Thee cittee mourneth the lack of a counsalor holsoom ;
And thee countrye moneth thee want of a zealus vpholder :
Vertu eeke lamenteth thee lack of an holye repentaunt.
How beyt dame Vertu thy goodnesse kindlye rewardeth,
In memory thin honour, thy soul eeke in glorye reposing.

VPON THEE DEATH OF THEE

right honourable thee *Lord Girald fitz Girald L. Baron*
of *Offalye*, who deceased at *S. Albans* in thee yeere
1580, thee last of Iune, thee xxj. yeere of his adge.

Oomtyme liu'lye *Girald* in graue now liu'les is
harbourd.
A matchlesse gallant, in byrth and auncetrye nobil.
His nobil linnadge *Kyldacr* with *Mountcguc* warrants.
Proper in his person, with gyfts so hym nature adorned.
In valor and in honor wel knowne too no man vnequal.
And a true sound subiect, to his Prince most faythful abyding.
Theese not with standing his liefe too to hastelye vannisht.

Nipt were thee blossooms, eare fruictful season aproched.
Wherefor his acquayntaunce his death so vntymelye
    bewayleth.
Maynoth lamenteth, *Kilka* and *Rathangan* ar howling.
Nay rather is mated bye this hard hap desolat *Ireland.*
Such claps of batter that seally vnfortunat *Island.*
O that I thy prayses could wel decipher in order,
Lyke *Homer* or *Virgil*, lyke *Geffray Chauncer* in English.
Then would thy *Stanyhurst* in pen bee liberal holden.
Thee poët is barrayn, for prayse rich matter is offred.

    Heere percase *carpers* wyl twight his iollitye youthful.
Strong reason vnstrayned that weake obiection aunswers.
Hee must bee peerlesse who in yong yeers faultes abydeth.
Such byrds flee seldoom, such black swans scantlye be
    floating.
In world of mischiefe who finds such glorius angels ?
Soom stars passe oothers ; al perls doe not equalye luster.
Thee soundest wheatcorne with chaffy filthod is husked,
What shal I say further, this loare diuinitye telleth ;
Vertuus he liued, through grace that vertuus eended.
What may be then better, than a godly and gratius vpshot ?
Too *God* in al pietee, too *Prince* in dutye remayning.
Whearefor (woorthye *Girald*) syth thy eend was hertye
    repentaunce,
Thy soul *God* gladdeth with saincts in blessed *Olympus*,
Thogh tumbd bee carcasse in towne of martyred *Alban*.

His noble man, yf wee respect thee giftes that *God*
planted in hym, was doubtlesse ful of good partes.
Of disposition kind and loouing, easelye moooued, and
as soone appeased ; apt too al maner of actiuitye, coooueting
in ecche laudable enterprice not only too bee commendable,
but also surpassing. In wyt quick and pregnaunt, and of
good forecast, namely as far as his yeeres would beare : yeet

soomwhat wantonly geeuen, where too *Youth*, *Nobilitee* and
lewd coompanye dyd carrye him, the *one* sturring, thee *oother*
warranting, thee *third* easelye trayning aman of deeper
iudgment too such fond phantasyes, yf by *God* his gratious
guerdon hee bee not thee stronger garded.   But a litle
beefore his death hee beecame such a *changling*, as hee dyd
not only purchase thee commendacion of strangers, but also
bred admiration in his freendes, who greatlye reioyced, too
see so penitent and godly an alteration from vice to vertue.
In which tyme finding his conscience deepelye gauld with
thee owtragious oathes hee vsed too thunder owt in gamening,
hee made a few verses, as yt were his *cygnea oratio :* which,
not so much for thee mceter, as thee matter, I thinck good,
too bee diuulged *verbatim*, as I found theym, after his decease,
scribled with his owne hand.   And yf thee *reader* hap too
stumble at thee vnderstanding of any *staffe*, let yt bee
sufficient, that thee *maker* his meaning was good.

A PENITENT SONNET WRIT-

ten by thee *Lord Girald* a litle

beefore his death.

B Y losse in play men oft forget
    Thee duitye they dooe owe,
Too hym that dyd bestow thee same,
    And thowsands millions moe.
I loathe too see them sweare and stare,
    When they the mayne haue lost ;
Forgetting al thee byes, that weare
    With God and holye goast.
By *wounds* and *nayles* they thinck to wyn,
    But truely yt is not so :
For al theyre frets and fumes in syn,
    They mooniles must goa.

Theare is no wight that vsd yt more,
   Than *hee* that wrote this verse ;
Who cryeth, *peccaui*, now therefore
   His othes his hert doe perce.
Therefor example take by *mee*,
   That curse thee lucklesse tyme ;
That eauer *dice* myn eyes dyd see,
   Which bred in mee this *crime*.
Pardon mee for that is past,
   I wyl offend no more :
In this moste vile and sinful *cast*,
   Which I wyl stil abhore.

AN EPITAPH ENTITVLED

Commune Defunctorum, such as oure vnlearned *Ryth-mours* accustomablye make vpon thee death of euery *Tom Tyler*, as yf yt were a *last* for euerye one his *foote*, in which thee quantitees of syllables are not too bee heeded.

Oom toe me, you *muses*, and thow most chieflye,
   Minerua,
   And ye that are dwellers in dens of darckned *Auerna* :
Help mye pen in wryting, a death moste soarye reciting,
Of the good old *Topas*, soon too thee mightye syr *Atlas*.
For grauitee the *Cato*, for wyt *Mars, Bacchus, Apollo* :
Scipio for warfare, for gentyl curtesye *Cæsar*.
A great *Alexander*, with a long whit neck lyke a *gaunder*.
In yeer's a *Nestor*, for wars a martial *Hector*,
Hannibal and *Pompey*, with *Tristam, Gallahad, Orckney* :
Hercules in coasting, a *Vulcan* mightelye toasting.
In wisdom *Salomon*, for streingth and currag a *Sampson*.

For iustice *Radamanthus*: in equitye woorthye *Lycurgus*.
And not a *Thersites*, but he was a subtil *Vlisses*.
In learning *Socrates*, in faythful freendship *Achates*.
Yea, thogh he stand namelesse, hee was in prowes *Achilles*.
A *Damon* and *Pythias*, for gould and siluer a *Midas*.
Noë for continuaunce, a lerned *Tullye* for vttraunce.
In trauayle *Æneas*, for secrets trustful *Iöllas*.
And in philosophy, a *Raymond*, a *Bacon*, a *Ripplye*.
In medicins *Pæon*, *Galen*, and most famosed *Alcon*,
Plinnye, *Dioscorides*, *Hipocrates*, and *Arafornes*,
O you cursd *Parcas*, why kyld ye the good soon of *Atlas*?
And whye, wythowt mercy, doe ye slea thee fayre ladye
    Thisbee.
A *Sara* for goodnesse, a great *Bellona* for hudgnesse.
For myldnesse *Anna*, for chastitye godlye *Susanna*.
Hester in a good shift, a *Iudith* stout at a dead lift.
Also *Iulietta*, with *Dido*, rich *Cleopatra*.
With sundry namelesse, and woomen more manye blamelesse.
Is not *he* wel garded, thee *wooman* richlye rewarded?

AN EPITAPH WRYTTEN BY SYR

Thomas More vpon thee death of *Henrye Abyngdon*,
one of thee gentlemen of thee *chappel*: which deuise
thee author was fayne too put in *meeter*, by reason
thee partye that requested his trauaile, dyd not lyke
of a verye proper *Epitaph* that was first framd,
beecause yt ran not *in rythme*, as may appeere at ful
in his *Latin Epigrammes*: where vpon Syr *Thomas
More*, shapte theese verses ensuing, with which the
suppliant was exceedinglye satisfyed, as yf thee
author had hyt thee nayle on thee head.

*Ic iacet* Henricus, *semper pietatis* amicus:
Nomen Abyngdon erat, *si quis sua nomina* quærat:
Wellis hic ecclesia *fuerat succentor in* alma,
Regis et in bella *cantor fuit ipse* capella.
Millibus in mille *cantor fuit optimus* ille.
Præter et hæc ista *fuit optimus* orgaquenista.
Nunc igitur Christe, *quoniam tibi seruijt* iste,
Semper in orbe soli *da sibi regna* poli.

The same thogh not *verbatim* construed, yeet in effect thus
may bee translated, wherein thee learned are not too looke
for thee exact obseruation of *quantitees* of *syllables*, which thee
authour in the *Latin* dyd not verye preciselye keepe.

Eere lyeth old *Henry*, no freend to mischeuus *enuye.*
Surnamd *Abyngdon*, to al men most hertelye *welcoom.*
Clerk he was in *wellis*, where tingle a great manye
bellis.
Also in thee *chappel* hee was not counpted a *moungrel:*
And such a lowd *singer*, in a thowsand not such a *ringer.*
And with a *concordance*, a man moste skilful in *organce.*
Now God I craue *duly:* sence this man saru'd the soe
truelye,
Henrye place in *kingdoom*,, that is also named *Abyngdon.*

FINIS.

IOHN PATES PRINTER
TO THEE CVRTEOVS READER.

Am too craue thy pacience and paynes (good reader) in bearing wyth such faultes as haue escapte in printing ; and in correcting as wel such as are layd downe heere too thy view, as al oother whereat thow shalt hap too stumble in perusing this treatise.   Thee nooueltye of im-printing English in theese partes, and thee absence of the author from perusing soom proofes could not choose but breede errours.   But for thee abridging of thy trauayle I wyl lay downe such faultes as are at this present found too bee of greatest importaunce.   And as for thee wrong placing of an V for an N, or an N for an V, and in printing two EE for one E, or one for two, and for thee mispoyncting of periods ; thee correction of theese I must bee forced for this tyme too refer too thye friendlye paynes.

FAVLTES.	CORRECTION.	
In thee dedicatorye epistle.		
Pag. 1. lin. 4 Endevvours,	reade, Endeuours.	[*p.* 3.]
lin. 22. ac.	as.	[*p.* 3.]
Page 3. lin. 32. cooke in soom copyes.	booke.	[*p.* 6.]

[The final leaf (unnumbered, but forming the 67th leaf of the Leyden edition of 1582) contains printing only on its first page.

This final leaf is wanting in the Ashburnham copy, and is supplied from the Britwell copy, which is however torn at the top.]

FAVLTES.		CORRJECTION.	
Pag. 4.	[lin.	]e beene	[*p.* .]
	lin	]ing.	[*p.* .]
Pag. 5.	lin. 31 frynig pan	fryi]ng pan.	[*p.* 9.]
Pag.	lin.	]e Reader.	[*p.* .]
	lin.	]seth.	[*p.* .]
Pag. 8.	lin. 28. Ortôgraghy]	Ortôgraphy.	[*p.* 13.]
Pag.	lin.	]laying.	[*p.* .]
Pag.	lin.	]sceing.	[*p.* .]
Pag. 2.	lin. 11. m]ishing.	missing.	[*p.* 18.]
	lin. [36.] rang.	randge.	[*p.* 19.]
Pag. 17.	lin. 6. sanckt.	sank.	[*p.* 36.]
	lin. 25. vvilde.	vvyde.	[*p.* 37.]
Pag. 19.	lin. 22. Endevvours.	endeuours.	[*p.* 39.]
Pag. 23.	lin. 29. vvith his chaapt staf,	vvith chaapt staf.	[*p.* 45.]
Pag. 25.	lin. 1. choloricque.	Cholericque.	[*p.* 46.]
	lin. 33. sacrafice.	sacrifice.	[*p.* 47.]
Pag. 36.	lin. 22. shavv Priamus	savv Priamus.	[*p.* 60.]
Pag. 38.	lin. 13. woonman.	vvooman.	[*p.* 62.]
Pag. 41.	lin. 13. assijtaunce	Assistaunce.	*p.* 65.]
	lin. 36. progeniotours.	progenitours.	[*p.* 66.]
Pag. 54.	lin. 26. desolat angel.	desolat angle.	[*p.* 81.]
Pag. 60.	lin. 18. fyrd Sicil.	fyerd Sicil.	[*p.* 88.]
Pag. 63.	lin. 36. A folck moaste.	A folck moate. 1. a coompanye, an assembly	[*p.* 92.]
Pag. 106.	lin. 24. Faultes abydeth.	Faultles abydeth.	[*p.* 152.]

Imprinted at Leiden in Holland by Iohn Pates. Anno M.D LXXXII.

THE FIRST
FOVRE BOOKES
OF VIRGILS ÆNEIS,

Translated into English Heroicall Verse,
by RICHARD STANYHURST:

With other Poëticll deuises
thereto annexed.

AT LONDON,

Imprinted by Henry Bynneman
dwelling in Thames streate neare
vnto Baynardes Castell.

ANNO DOMINI,
1583.

THE PRINTER TO THE
Curteous Reader.

 Am to craue thy pacience (good Reader) and thy friendly acceptaunce of my paines in printing this booke. The noueltye of the verse, and the absence of the Author put me halfe in a feare either to displease the gentlemen that penned it, or not to please the gentlemen that reade it: if I should obserue the newe Ortographie vsed in the booke, (whether with the writers mind, or the Printers fault, I know not) it might haue bred error in the vnderstanding of many, and misliking in the iudgement of most. And very loth I am to seeme vniurious to the Author, in straying any whit from his prescribed rules in writing, exactly obseruing the quantity of each syllable. If I haue here and there changed some one or other letter, My purpose was to giue more light to the matter, by that maner of speech, whereto our country men are most acqainted. The absence of any letter, which for the necessitie of the verse often falleth out, I haue noted with an Apostrophe thus (') [:] for the placing of two oo and ee for one, and contrary one for two, which thou mayst often meete with in reading, I am to refer thee to the Authors Epistle at the beginning and generally to commend to thy curtesie my trauaile in so straunge and vnaccustomed a worke.

www.ingramcontent.com/pod-product-compliance
Lightning Source LLC
Chambersburg PA
CBHW031112020726
47495CB00007B/2164